DADDY BEAR

LAYLAH ROBERTS

Laylah Roberts

Daddy Bear

© 2019, Laylah Roberts

Laylah.roberts@gmail.com

laylahroberts.com

Cover Design by: Allycat Designs

Editing: Celeste Jones

❀ Created with Vellum

LET'S KEEP IN TOUCH!

Don't miss a new release, sign up to my newsletter for sneak peeks, deleted scenes and giveaways: https://landing.mailerlite.com/webforms/landing/p7l6go

I also have a readers group on Facebook if you want to join: https://www.facebook.com/groups/386830425069911/

BOOKS BY LAYLAH ROBERTS

Doms of Decadence

Just for You, Sir

Forever Yours, Sir

For the Love of Sir

Sinfully Yours, Sir

Make me, Sir

A Taste of Sir

To Save Sir

Sir's Redemption

Reveal Me, Sir

Old-Fashioned Series

An Old-Fashioned Man

Two Old-Fashioned Men

Her Old-Fashioned Husband

Her Old-Fashioned Boss

His Old-Fashioned Love

An Old-Fashioned Christmas

Haven, Texas Series

Lila's Loves

Laken's Surrender

Saving Savannah

Molly's Man

Saxon's Soul

Mastered by Malone

How West Was Won

Montana Daddies

Daddy Bear

Daddy's Little Darling

Daddy's Naughty Darling (in Dirty Daddies Anthology)

Daddy's Sweet Girl

Daddy's Lost Love

A Montana Daddies Christmas

Daring Daddy

Wildeside

Wilde

Sinclair

Luke

The Hunters

A Mate to Cherish

A Mate to Sacrifice

Men of Orion

Worlds Apart

Cavan Gang

Rectify

Redemption

Redemption Valley

Audra's Awakening

1

She was so lost.

Ellie gripped the steering wheel so tight her fingers ached as she stared out at the snow-covered road. This was not good. Not good at all.

Her car wasn't equipped to handle these conditions. Hell, *she* wasn't equipped to handle these conditions. She was from Miami, she wasn't used to snow.

At least the heater in her car worked, but if she didn't get to her aunt's place soon, she was going to be in real trouble. She was so scared. She didn't have a clue about how to drive in these conditions.

She flicked a quick glance at the gas gauge. She'd put twenty dollar's worth of gas in this morning, thinking that would be enough. But she hadn't counted on getting stuck in a damn snow storm.

Why hadn't she checked the weather forecast? She should have waited this storm out somewhere safe before continuing on.

Right. And what sort of motel was she going to find that cost around forty-eight dollars and ninety-cents? 'Cause that's all she had left of the money she'd taken when she'd left her parents' house.

She still felt guilty about that and damn it, she shouldn't. How long had she put her life on hold to take care of them? They had lied to her. Deceived her. Fuck, how could she have been so damn naïve?

Her eyes filled with tears, their betrayal still raw and cutting. She needed to stop being such a pushover. She'd spent years of her life looking after others. Putting herself last. Doing what she thought was her duty, because they were her parents and they loved her.

You owe us, Ellen.

If you walk out that door you are nothing to us. Don't ever come back.

A sob welled in her chest. Hadn't she done enough crying already? They didn't deserve her tears.

You are no longer our daughter.

It was time to take charge of her life. She was twenty-three years old and she'd never had sex. Hell, she'd never even been on a proper date. And her last kiss had been from Boomer Marston in the back of his pick-up. He'd managed to get his hand up her top to squeeze her breast.

It hadn't exactly been a first kiss to remember. But it was all she had. What would her life be like if she hadn't done as her parents ordered and broken things off with him?

She could be Mrs. Boomer Palmer. She grimaced. Eleanor Palmer. Yuck. Would she and Boomer now have a passel of little Boomers and Boomettes running around? She risked letting go of the steering wheel to quickly wipe at her face, her vision blurring with tears. She needed to pull herself together.

She turned a corner of the road and a cry escaped her as her heart went into overdrive. A huge tree blocked the road and she was headed straight towards it. Reaching instinctively, she slammed her foot on the brakes.

Her car fishtailed, unable to gain traction on the icy road. It spun, sliding towards the side of the road. Large trees loomed, looking menacing in the near dark and she frantically turned the wheel, trying to get her car back under control. It didn't respond. The car smashed into a tree, coming to a brutal stop. Her head snapped forward, slamming against the steering wheel. Her vision blurred, blackness creeping around her vision as she slipped into unconsciousness.

BEAR STUDIED the deteriorating weather and knew it would be foolish to attempt to make it back to the ranch tonight. Using the Bluetooth system, he put a call through to the security center at Sanctuary.

"Sanctuary Ranch, you're talking with Corbin."

He kept his gaze on the road, dropping his speed slightly. Things were getting ugly out here.

"It's Bear. Not gonna make it back tonight."

Sanctuary had been his home since he was a child. When he'd left school, it had felt natural to stay on and work there. He'd never had the desire to go anywhere else. It was where people accepted him, his desires, his needs. Because the people who lived and worked there shared his views. There was a special set of criteria anyone hired on had to fulfill.

Clint Jensen ran the ranch that his great-great-grandfather had set up with his brother. They'd wanted a place where they could live in peace with their wife. Who they shared. Back then, that must have caused a huge stir and he couldn't blame them for wanting to shelter their wife from any ridicule.

They'd only allowed like-minded people to join them on the

ranch. Men who wanted a different sort of relationship. Men who believed that women should be sheltered, coddled and taken in hand when necessary. Clint had followed in his great-great-grand-father's shoes.

Bear didn't know if he'd ever be able to fall in love again. He'd been burned once. He'd thought himself in love and it turned out she'd only been using him. She'd lied to him. Deceived him.

"Roger that," Corbin replied. "Where are you at?"

Bear looked around him. "I'm about an hour south of the ranch but the snow is coming down fast. Not much point in carrying on. I'm going to head to the cabin."

Clint's dad had built a cabin not too far from the ranch for the times he wanted to get away for a bit of solitude with his wife. Bear had used it a time or two himself when he'd wanted to do some hunting.

He'd already passed the first turn-off that lead to the cabin, but there was another road up further he could take. He turned the corner, immediately saw a huge tree blocking the road.

"Shit!"

"Bear? Everything okay?" Corbin's voice lacked its earlier lazy tone. Now he was all business.

He didn't answer, his heart racing as he spotted the car off to one side, the front of it crumpled where it had crashed against another big tree.

"Fuck! There's a tree blocking the road. A car has crashed into it, I'm going to stop and check there's no one inside."

And if there is, please let them be alive.

He gradually took his foot off the accelerator, slowing down. He hadn't been going very fast, and luckily, he'd put his snow tires on his truck the other day.

"Let me know what's going on and if you need help," Corbin replied calmly. "I'll let Clint and Kent know what's happened. I'll also alert the authorities about the tree blocking the road."

"Got it. Will check in soon."

He left his truck running, switched on the hazards in case anyone came around the corner behind him, although most sane people wouldn't be out in this weather. He pulled on some gloves and grabbed his jacket, dragging it on before stepping out. Bear moved around the truck and opened up the storage unit he kept in the back. It contained a flashlight, an emergency foil blanket and a first aid kit along with a shovel and some flares. He grabbed the flashlight, since it was growing darker.

He liked to be prepared.

"Hello?" he called out as he approached the other vehicle. "Anyone in the car?"

It had stopped running. He wondered how long it had been sitting here.

"Hello?"

No answer. Shit. He had a bad feeling about this. He moved to the driver's side first and peered in.

A woman lay slumped over the steering wheel, her dark hair around her face. She wasn't moving. He quickly ran the flashlight over the rest of the car but didn't see anyone else. He opened the driver's door.

"Sweetheart, can you hear me?"

Nothing. He wrenched off a glove and pulled back some of her soft hair, pressing his fingers against her neck. Relief filled him as he felt her pulse. It was a bit too slow for his liking though, and she was freezing cold. He needed to assess her quickly then get her into the warmth of his truck.

She was a little bit of a thing with curly dark hair flowing everywhere and dressed in jeans and a sweater. No jacket. No hat or scarf. Was it safe to move her? Hell, he didn't have much choice. If he didn't, the cold was going to kill her.

He gently pushed her back against the seat, wincing as he saw the big, egg-shaped lump on her forehead. At least she had her seatbelt on. No air bags, though.

Jesus if she was his...well, she wasn't so no point in thinking about that.

He slipped an arm under her legs and one around her back and slid her out of the seat and up into his arms. She let out a small cry and he tensed, waiting for her to awaken, but she just pushed her face against his chest and went limp once more.

Urgency filled him. He needed to get her to the cabin and warmed up.

He moved swiftly over to his truck and placed her on the bench seat. She looked like a little doll in his big truck. How old was she? He didn't think the top of her head would even reach his shoulders.

Whoever was meant to be looking after her wasn't doing a very good job, letting her go out in weather like this, wearing a thin sweater and in a crap car that couldn't handle the conditions.

He did up her belt then shut the door, moving to the back of his truck to grab the blanket. He returned and tucked it around her. She was slumped over. Frowning, he undid the belt and lifted her over into the middle. Now she could lean against him and he could stop her from jolting around more and hurting herself.

He returned to her car to get her belongings. There was just a small, battered suitcase in the trunk and a handbag in the front passenger seat.

Who was she and what was she doing out here on her own?

2

She was so warm.

It felt so good she might have snuggled in and gone back to sleep if it wasn't for the agony in her head. She raised her hand up, trying to push the heavy covers away. Just how many blankets did she have on her?

She touched her forehead and whimpered as pain radiated through her head.

"Uh-uh, don't touch your injury, little one. You'll make it hurt more."

The voice was deep, a little rough. Like autumn leaves rustling together. She went still.

Who the hell was that?

"And you need to keep your hands under the covers. Stay warm. Your temperature got too low and we need to keep you covered up." A large, warm hand grasped hers and gently tucked it back under the blankets.

Temperature? Covered up? Injury? Had the owner of that voice hurt her?

No, wait. She remembered driving. Snow. Downed tree. She'd

been in a car accident. So where was she now? And who did that voice belong to? She didn't want to open her eyes. Because she was pretty certain she hadn't found her way to a hospital and that wasn't a friendly male nurse.

But the voice sounded kind. When was the last time anyone cared about whether she was warm or not? Hell, she couldn't remember.

So deciding to be brave, she forced her eyes open. Her vision was blurred and it took her a few blinks to bring her sight into focus. She was lying in bed, blankets piled around her. There was a bit of a musty smell, as though the place needed a good airing out. But the mattress was comfortable.

There was movement to her right and she turned her head carefully, not wanting to risk making her head pound any more than it was. She stilled as she saw the man sitting on an armchair next to the bed.

He was enormous. Thick, wide shoulders were covered in a checked shirt. The sleeves were rolled up to the elbows revealing large forearms. His hands were big and battered, not smooth like Boomer's had been. These were the hands of a man who worked for a living.

Dark jeans covered his legs, although she couldn't see below his knees. Finally, she forced herself to look up. He had a neatly trimmed dark beard. Funny, she'd never thought of beards as attractive, but it seemed to suit him. His wasn't a handsome face. It was a bit too hard, his features a touch too pronounced to be considered handsome. But it was a face you wouldn't soon forget.

Dark eyes studied her. At first, they appeared to be almost black, but she realized they were actually a deep shade of brown. His chestnut-colored hair was brushed back off his face.

She blushed as she realized she'd been staring at him. He hadn't moved. He simply watched her back. She needed to say something. Maybe ask him who he was or how she'd come to be here. Was this his cabin? Did he live here alone? Was he some kind of mountain man? Yep, she had a hundred questions. She just didn't know where to start. She opened her mouth.

"Hi."

Wow. Well done, Ellie. In high school, she'd gotten into trouble repeatedly for not being able to keep quiet and all she had to say was hi.

His lips twitched. Great. She'd amused him. Woo hoo.

"How many fingers am I holding up?" he asked, putting three fingers up a few inches in front of her eyes.

"Ten," she answered without thinking.

His eyes widened, alarm filling his face.

"Sorry," she said quickly. "I've got a weird sense of humor sometimes. It was three."

He frowned. "Your health isn't a joke, little miss."

A shiver of what felt suspiciously like desire went through her. She didn't find that low, gravelly voice arousing, did she?

Nope. Not her. She was not looking for a man. Certainly not a dominant one. She wanted to be on her own. Make her own decisions. Her own plans. She did not want to be stuck dancing to someone else's tune.

She cleared her throat. "Umm, sorry. I will try not to joke about my health in the future. Unless I'm dying then all bets are out the window."

He scowled. All right. He really didn't appreciate her attempt at humor.

"I'm Ellie."

He inclined his head. Why did she feel like he already knew that?

"Hi Ellie, I'm Bear Macall."

"Bear? Really? That's your name? That's cool, I like it," she said quickly. She didn't want to insult him. Was it his real name? His lips twitched. Okay, she was back to being funny.

"Your driver's license says your name is Eleanor Margaret Bantler. You prefer Ellie, though?"

The only people who called her Eleanor were her parents. She didn't want to be called Eleanor anymore. She wanted a fresh start.

"My name is Ellie," she said firmly. Then she stiffened, a slight frisson of fear going through her. "How do you know what my driver's license says? Did you go through my wallet?"

What about her money? Had he taken it? It wasn't much, but it was all she had.

And you probably owe him that and more for rescuing you, Ellie. Shit.

"I did. I wanted to see if there was any information about your health in your bags that I might need to know to take care of you properly. You banged your head against the steering wheel when you crashed your car. Don't know how long you were sitting there before I found you, but when I arrived your car was out of gas." He gave her a look filled with disapproval. "And your skin was cold. Much longer and hypothermia would have gotten you."

"Oh. Well. Thank you. Umm and you brought me back here? To your place?" She tried to surreptitiously feel around to see if she was still dressed. Her hand brushed against her jeggings and she had to hold back a sigh of relief. He seemed like a nice guy but you could never be too careful. Ellie knew she wasn't the best judge of character. She was too trusting.

"This ain't my place. It's a cabin my boss owns. I live on a ranch about an hour from here."

"Oh. Right. Were you on your way there when you came across me? You couldn't get through because of that tree either?"

"Already decided to head here. Snow was coming down too hard. Still is." He turned and looked out the window. She couldn't see much in this position so she attempted to lean up on her elbow, groaning as her head protested.

He turned swiftly back to her, standing and looming over her in such a way that she gasped and fell back against the bed with a cry of pain.

"Jesus, little one. Don't move like that. You'll hurt yourself."

"To-too late." Tears fell down her cheeks as agony engulfed her. The room spun slightly, making her feel ill.

"Easy, now. I'm sorry I frightened you. I shouldn't have moved so quickly." His voice was a soft croon. She'd expected him to scold her and instead he was taking the blame.

"No. My fault," she told him. "I just...I was trying to look out the window and when you turned...I just got a bit of a fright. Sorry."

She forced herself to look up as he grimaced. "Nothing to be sorry for, little one. I tend to scare most women, but I want you to know I would never hurt you, all right? You don't need to fear me or my size."

She wasn't truly afraid, it had just been instinctive. After all, she didn't really know him.

He turned away. "I'm going to go and get some more firewood. When I come back in, I'll make you some soup."

"You cook?" she asked. More to get him to linger than anything else. He seemed almost hurt by her reaction. But that was silly, he didn't know her any better than she knew him. He put on his jacket and turned back to give her a smile without once meeting her gaze.

"I can cook. But in this case, it's just canned stuff I'm afraid."

"That's all right. I'm used to canned soup."

"You are?"

"Yeah. I'm a terrible cook. My mother used to say that if it was possible to burn water, I would."

"Your mom? Will she be worried about you? I have my sat phone, we could try to call her." Now he was looking straight at her, concern in his gaze.

"That's okay. I don't need to call her."

He frowned slightly. "Someone else?"

"No. There's no one to call," she said quietly. "Some soup would be good, though. Thank you."

She moved her gaze back to the ceiling and eventually she heard the door open. A gust of cold wind rocked its way through the cabin but it was quickly gone as the door closed again.

And she was alone. Which was a good thing. There was nothing wrong with being on your own. It meant that you got to make all the decisions. Eat what you want. Go to bed when you liked. Be whoever you wanted to be.

So why did the thought of being alone scare her half to death?

BEAR STRODE out of the cabin and headed to the small shack at the side where the firewood was stored. He'd have to come back when the weather was a bit better and restock supplies. But for now, he was glad that there was already a pile of firewood chopped and ready. He'd already brought in an armload earlier when he'd lit the fire. But he wanted to stock up. He started piling it up next to the door, under the porch roof.

Plus, he'd needed an excuse to get away from the small woman tucked up in the only bed in the cabin. He didn't think she'd realized that yet. But then she probably wasn't thinking clearly.

Why had she been driving around in the middle of a snow storm? And why didn't she have anyone to call?

A little thing like her should be coddled. She should have someone watching over her and making certain that she stayed safe.

That she apparently didn't have that didn't sit well with him at all.

He brought the last armload inside. He'd just opened the door when he heard a pained cry, followed by a thump. Dropping the armload of wood where he stood, he flicked the door shut and raced towards the bed that was partially screened off from what was essentially a one-room cabin with a small attached bathroom.

He found her lying on the floor in a heap, her hands grasping her head as though she thought it might roll right off her neck. She probably wished it would, considering how much that fall had to have hurt her.

He needed to get some painkillers into her, but he hadn't wanted to give her anything until she'd woken up. How the hell had she managed to fall out? The bed was high, she could have really hurt herself. Did he need to fashion some sort of railing for her?

His first instinct was to pick her up and put her back into bed. But he remembered her reaction to him earlier. It wasn't that he blamed her, but Bear was the last person to ever harm a woman. Sure, he wouldn't hesitate to spank his woman if she ever disobeyed him and put herself in danger. But that was a small hurt to prevent a greater harm. It was the way he'd been raised. His father spanked his mother.

He crouched down, trying to make himself smaller and kept a few feet between them.

"Little miss? You okay? Did you hurt yourself?" She was such a tiny thing. Especially in comparison to him. Gorgeous too. With pale skin and wide, blue eyes and all that crazy hair which was a riot of curls around her face.

She was adorable. His cock stirred, reminding him how long it had been since he'd had a woman. He was becoming a monk.

But he shouldn't be thinking of her in a sexual way. For one, she was a stranger. Two, she was injured. Three, she was scared of him.

Not a good combination.

"Did you fall out of bed?"

She groaned and removed one hand. "Head hurts. So much. Going to be sick."

He scooped her up. He didn't have time to ask permission to touch her, her health came before anything else. He got her to the toilet just in time as she started vomiting. Thank God Clint had indoor plumbing installed in the cabin a few years back.

He held her against him, one hand holding back those curls, the other wrapped gently around her hips as she heaved and shuddered. Finally, she stopped throwing up, slumping against him as though she just didn't have the energy to hold herself up. And he was certain she didn't. He gently sat her on the floor, so she was leaning against the wall. Then he flushed the toilet.

He grabbed a clean face cloth from the small storage cupboard under the sink and wet it before crouching before her, holding it out. But she either didn't see it or didn't have the energy to grab it so he gently grasped hold of her chin, carefully raising her face up to wash it.

He was shocked to find tears running down her cheeks.

"Baby girl, are you hurting? As soon as I get you back into bed, I'll get you some pain killers. Are you allergic to anything?"

"I'm sorry. I'm so sorry. I can't believe I did that. That was so gross. And you had to hold me through it and see that. I'm so sorry. I'm such a bother."

That was why she was upset? Because he'd seen her vomiting? Because he'd taken care of her? Hell, looking after her was a privilege not a chore as far as he was concerned.

"Ellie. Ellie, look at me." He waited until those blue eyes stared up at him. They were cloudy with pain and tears continued to drip down her cheeks. He reached back and grabbed some toilet paper then bundled it up and wiped her nose.

She started to sob. "Oh God, and now you're having to wipe my nose. What next? My bottom?"

"Hey. Hey, listen to me now."

Her gaze turned down once more.

Nope. That wasn't happening. "Little girl, you listen to me right now or you're going to find yourself in trouble." She wasn't his and he had no right to reprimand her. But he didn't want her feeling bad about this. She raised her gaze slowly, wincing in pain.

"I am not worried about taking care of you while you vomit or have a running nose or even if you need help using the toilet, understand me?"

"But you don't even know me," she wailed.

"Maybe not. But you need me. And I want to help you."

"You cannot tell me you like cleaning up someone else's vomit?"

He grinned. "Nope, can't tell you that. However, I do like taking care of little girls."

She snorted. "Everyone must seem little to you. How tall are you?"

"Six-five." He tensed, waiting for any sign of fear but none came.

"I'm still really sorry," she told him. "I thought I could make it to the toilet and back on my own, but when I stood up the room started to spin and then I fell and my head jolted and I thought it was going to explode. I think that's why I vomited. It still feels like there are shards of glass being pounded into my head. I could really use those painkillers."

He frowned. "You got out of bed? You didn't fall?"

"Fall? No. I haven't fallen out of bed since I was five and had a nightmare that monsters were chasing me." She shuddered. "That was awful."

"Monsters are scary," he said solemnly. "Luckily, daddies are good at scaring them away."

"Huh. My dad told me to go back to bed and stop being silly."

What kind of father would say that to his little girl? He'd never say that to his girl, big or small.

"So why didn't you wait for me to come back to take you to the toilet? From now on, you don't go anywhere without my help, understand?"

"What if you're not here?" She was blushing bright red. It was pretty cute.

"I won't be far away."

She opened her mouth and he put up his hand to still any more arguments. "And if I have to go out for longer or you're worried about not being able to hold on, well, we'll sort something out. I'm sure I could fashion some sort of diaper."

He hid his smile at her shocked gasp. He probably shouldn't have said that. He half-expected her to slap him or tell him he was a sick asshole, instead she just gaped at him.

"I don't think so!"

"Let's get you on the toilet and then back to bed." He glanced from her to the toilet. Grabbing her before had been a necessity, but he didn't want to frighten her.

"Do I have your permission to help you?"

She stared up at him in confusion. "You just threatened to put me in a diaper and told me I better not get out of bed without your help and now you're asking my permission to help me?"

He grimaced. "Yeah, well, I don't want you moving without help. I can't risk you hurting yourself further. But I also know you're scared of me and I don't want to just grab you."

"I'm not scared of you." She looked at him in surprise.

"You shied away from me earlier."

"You gave me a fright. And you are big. And a stranger. But I don't think someone who is out to hurt me would be upset at the idea I might fall and harm myself. Or have held me while I vomited."

"You don't know that, little miss," he told her. "I could still have an ulterior motive. You shouldn't be so trusting."

"Are you trying to talk me out of trusting you?"

What was he doing? He sighed. "You can trust me. But I don't want you to think that just because a stranger is kind that he is a good person."

She closed her eyes and leaned back against the wall. Seemed she really did trust him if she was willing to take her gaze off him. Or maybe she was just in that much pain.

"I know I'm too trusting and naïve. I've been told that over and over."

Who told her that? He didn't like the sad note to her voice.

"Nothing wrong with being naïve and trusting, so long as you have someone to watch over you and make sure you're not taken advantage of," he told her gruffly.

She opened her eyes with a small smile, but he could see how pale she was, her mouth was pinched. She was in a lot of pain and he was here lecturing her on trusting people.

"Wouldn't it be nice to have someone like that?" she said wistfully.

"Ellie, do I have your permission to take care of you while you're here? I promise I won't take advantage in any way."

Her gaze met his. "I have a choice?"

He sighed. "Not really. Snow's still coming down hard and I can tell you're in a lot of pain. You're not up to looking after yourself right now and I'm all you've got. Sorry."

"Don't be sorry." She reached up a hand and patted her cheek. "I've never had anyone take care of me before. Might not know you...but it's kind of nice."

She was fading fast, her energy completely depleted.

"So, you're okay with me taking care of you as I see fit?"

She gave him a suspicious look. "You're not going to diaper me, are you?"

His lips twitched. "Not unless it becomes necessary." Then he gave her a stern look. "But if it's necessary for your health, it will happen."

She snorted. "You have a weird sense of humor too."

No, he didn't. Because he wasn't joking. But he didn't think it was necessary to argue that point with her right now. He reached out and clasped hold of her hand. She was freezing. He took her pulse.

"Little one?"

"Yes, you have my permission to take care of me. You know, it sounds nice, which is weird 'cause I want to be the one making the decisions, or so I thought."

She was half-asleep. He knew she probably wouldn't have admitted any of that if she'd been fully aware of what was going on. He slipped an arm under her legs and carefully picked her up. He remembered that she hadn't been to the toilet yet. This was going to be slightly awkward. He really hoped she remembered later on that she had given him permission to look after her. He pushed the lid of the toilet down and sat on it, arranging her on his lap. Then he reached for the zip on her jeans and realized they didn't have one.

"What sort of denim is this?" he asked. They were so thin, he could pretty much put his finger through it.

"They're jeggings," she said with a yawn. "Leggings that look like jeans."

"How the hell are they supposed to keep you warm?"

"I'm from Florida. Not used to all this damn snow."

"You should have warm clothing, a proper jacket, socks, boots, gloves, a hat."

"Yes, Daddy," she teased. He felt a surge of pleasure. She didn't have a clue what that word did to him.

He lifted her up and pulled the jeggings off. He figured he might as well pull them completely off. Easier than doing it each time she needed to pee. He reached for panties. They were white with little pink hearts. Cute.

"What you doin'?" she slurred, patting at his hand ineffectively.

"You can't go to the toilet with your panties on."

He waited for a protest.

"Oh, yeah." She giggled. "Guess not."

She definitely wasn't with it. He slid them down and left them around her knees then he stood and raised the seat, placing her down. He had to hold her steady or she would have fallen right off. She was practically asleep. She just sat there, doing nothing. Every so often a shiver racked her body. Damn it. He needed to get her back under the covers and warm.

"Ellie? Baby girl, you need to go." He ran his hand down her back, trying to wake her up enough to get her to pee.

"Go where? Don't wanna go. Like it here with you." She wrapped her arms around his waist and hugged him. He stood still. Shocked. His cock hardened even as his heart softened. Stupid. He didn't know her. Plus, as soon as she could take care of herself, she'd be out of here.

"So cuddly. You're just like my own giant teddy bear."

She hadn't just said that, had she? He shook his head. If Clint or Kent could see him now...well, they'd probably be jealous as fuck.

He and Clint shared the same interests. Both of them were Daddy Doms. Kent was a Dom as well, he wanted a woman who would be submissive to him, who would allow him to lead.

"Had a teddy bear once," she muttered.

Once? Where had it gone?

"My aunt gave it to me. Well, my great-aunt. I loved that bear."

"Did you lose it, baby?" he asked gently.

"My mom threw it out. Said I was too old for it anymore." He stilled his gentle massage. What the hell?

"How old were you?"

"Four," she sighed. "I like when you touch me. His name was Jeremiah."

"What?" he asked in surprise.

"The bear. His name was Jeremiah. I loved him. Wish I had him right now. Guess it's good I've got you, huh?"

"Yeah, baby, it is." Sounded like she could use someone to put her needs first. What had her parents been thinking of? First her father telling her not to be silly because she'd had a nightmare then her mother throwing away her teddy bear. He'd just have to get her another one...he pushed that thought away. He wouldn't be able to do that because he wouldn't see her once he got her back to civilization and a hospital.

"Baby, you need to pee. Here, this might help." He took a step back to turn on the tap.

She squeezed him tight. "Don't leave me!"

"Hey, shh," he soothed. "I'm not going anywhere." He turned the tap on. "I can't run the water for long but this might help." Within seconds he heard her pee and sighed in relief. He turned off the tap, grabbed some toilet paper and wiped her dry before pulling her up. He held her against him with one arm while he awkwardly pulled up her panties. Then he carried her back into the bedroom and tucked her under the covers.

He moved back into the bathroom and quickly cleaned his hands before reaching into the cupboard to grab the medical kit. It was well stocked. He brought it back into the main area of the cabin and sat on the armchair he'd moved next to the bed, resting the kit on the mattress next to Ellie.

Ellie had her eyes closed, her face pale. She still looked in pain. And that wasn't acceptable.

"Are you allergic to any pain killers, Ellie?" he asked her.

"N-no."

Shivers wracked her body, making her whimper. Shit. He hoped she wasn't getting ill. He placed the back of his hand over her forehead. Did she feel a bit warm? He wasn't sure. He looked down at the two thermometers. One was the normal sort that went in your mouth. The other was one that was slid into a little girl's bottom. He couldn't use that on her. It was one thing to help her to the toilet, but she wasn't his.

He grabbed the oral thermometer.

"Open up, Ellie. I need to take your temperature."

She opened her mouth instantly. He slipped it into her mouth. Christ, he was a sick asshole for finding it a turn on that she obeyed so beautifully.

Not yours, asshole.

He slid the thermometer out. Slightly elevated but not too bad. He stood and walked to the small kitchen and pulled a glass out of a cupboard. Then he looked back at her and changed his mind, he didn't want to sit her up so she could drink. He searched in the cupboards and came up with a child's sippy cup. It looked a bit old but it would do.

He filled it with water, then secured the lid. He returned to the armchair and grabbed a couple of painkillers from the first aid kit, holding them up to her mouth.

"Open up, Ellie. You need to swallow these."

"Don't wanna," she said sulkily.

He raised an eyebrow. This was the first hint of defiance he'd had from her and it surprised him. There was also a childish note to her voice that stirred things inside him. She wrinkled her nose. "Yucky."

He sighed. Didn't matter if she thought them yucky or not, she would be taking these. Because the alternative was her being in pain and that wasn't happening.

"Ellie, you open your mouth and swallow these like a good girl."

"Or what?" She opened her eyes to look up at him. "Aren't you suppose to add a threat to that statement?"

He shook his head. "I should. But you're certainly not well enough for a spanking."

She dropped her lip. "You'd spank me. That's mean." Okay, so that pout was adorable. But not so cute as to sway him.

"It's not mean. It's punishment for when you're naughty. If you don't want a spanking then don't be naughty."

She yawned. "I don't know if I want a spanking. It would probably hurt."

He raised an eyebrow. "That's kind of the point."

"You'd really hit me?"

"I would never hit you," he said fervently. "And I wouldn't spank you unless we had the sort of relationship where I was in charge. Where I would hold you accountable to my rules. And if you broke those rules or did something that put yourself in danger then I would spank your little butt. But we don't have that relationship. I don't have your agreement to be my submissive." He really shouldn't be having this conversation with her and certainly not in the dazed state she was in.

"Oh, you're a Dom."

He stared down at her in surprise. "You know what a Dom is?"

She snorted. "Duh. I read. I might be a virgin, but I'm not an idiot. Do you use whips and canes and stuff?" There was a note of fear in her voice.

"Not really into that."

"You have a dungeon? Some leathers? How did you get into it?" Her fatigue seemed to disappear as she grew more animated. "Or do you go to a club? Do they have BDSM clubs out here?"

"Do you always ask this many questions?"

She looked embarrassed. "Sorry. I know I talk a lot and it annoys people."

Shit, he hadn't meant to make her feel bad. "I don't have a dungeon and I very rarely go to a club. The closest one is about three hours drive away. Do you know what a Daddy Dom is?"

"No."

"Well, that's what I am. I want a certain kind of submissive. A big little girl who wants someone to coddle and protect her. To guide her. And to discipline her when necessary." And why was he telling her this? She should be swallowing her pills and going to sleep, not discussing his relationship preferences.

"Oh. So they would call you Daddy?" Her eyes drifted shut then open. She really needed sleep. "How does that work? Would she be Little all the time?

"Probably not all the time." He lowered his voice, hoping to lull her to sleep. "She'd have her big girl time too. It would depend on our relationship and what we were both comfortable with. I'd never make someone do anything they didn't wish to do. Littles come in all shapes and sizes."

"What do they do, when they're Little?"

"Depends on the Little and what age they associate with. Some like to color, to watch cartoons, to dress in princess clothes and have a tea party. Others like to have bottles and binkies. No one-size-fits-all."

She yawned, her eyes closing.

"Little girl, you need to take these pain killers then sleep."

"My father wasn't very loving. And he never really disciplined me. Maybe I'd like a Daddy Dom. Only I'm not looking for a relationship right now, sorry."

He hadn't been aware that he'd offered. He was attracted to her, though and it was obvious that she could use a keeper. But it couldn't go anywhere.

"Eleanor, if you're not going to swallow these pills—"

"I don't like being called Eleanor," she said in a soft voice. A tear dripped down her cheek. Shit. He hated seeing her cry. How had this woman come to mean so much in just a few hours?

Maybe it was because she was so helpless and that was a big trigger for him.

"Okay, sweetie. I won't call you Eleanor. But you really need these pills. If you're not going to swallow them, then I'll have to use the suppositories."

She cracked open an eye. "You'd stick them up my bottom?"

"Not these ones. I have some special suppository ones."

"I don't think I'd like that." She opened her mouth and he placed the pills on her tongue. Then he pressed the lip of the sippy cup in her mouth. She sucked down a few gulps of water.

"Drink a bit more."

"Tired. Don't want it."

"Okay, sleep now, little girl."

Bear watched her for a moment. He didn't like the nausea and drowsiness. He worried that she had a concussion. He would need to keep a close eye on her. He wished he could get her to the hospital, but they weren't going anywhere for a while

He settled himself in for a long night.

3

She placed her arm over her eyes, trying to shield them from the light assaulting them. She'd been having a nice dream about being hugged by a giant teddy bear when she'd been rudely awakened by this torture.

"Go away. Sleeping. Don't wanna get up."

"Honey, I've just got to check your pupils then you can sleep some more."

She tried to turn her head away but a sharp pain radiating through her head made her still, a cry escaping from her lips.

"Little girl, stay still," the stern voice told her. "This will only take a minute and I don't want you hurting yourself."

"Too late." Her stomach rolled sickeningly as the light went on and off. It felt like fireworks were going off behind her eyes and she groaned. "Don't feel well."

The light went away and a large hand landed over her forehead. "You don't feel warm, but I'll take your temperature again."

"I'm sick," she said miserably.

"Tell me if you're going to throw up, all right?"

"Don't like throwing up," she told him. "Yucky."

He snorted. "I don't think anyone likes throwing up." There was a rustling noise. "All right, open up."

She pressed her lips together stubbornly.

"Little girl, I've got a rectal thermometer in here, wouldn't take much for me to pull these covers down, bare your butt and push it up into your bottom."

She immediately opened her mouth. But even though she definitely didn't want anything going up her butt, her insides tingled at his words. What was with that?

He slid the thermometer back out. "Just a little elevated. I think it's the head injury making you feel sick. How is your pain level?"

She forced herself to open her eyes and stare up at him. Her rescuer. "It's okay," she said automatically.

"Okay, huh?" He gave her a chiding look.

She bit her lip. She was used to downplaying her own issues, because her parents had always been so ill. Seemed selfish to complain about bronchitis when your mom had cancer.

Except she hadn't had cancer. And Ellie had still been expected to take care of them while she was ill.

"Want to try that again?" he rumbled.

"My head is pretty sore."

"Good girl. That's better."

His praise filled her with warmth. What was it about this man that a word of praise meant so much to her? Was it because she'd had precious little praise in her life? She guessed so. But for some reason she wanted to know more about this man. "Is Bear your real name?"

He blushed slightly, surprising her. "No, it's not."

"What is it?"

He didn't answer her. Huh. That just made her feel nosier.

She took the painkillers he gave her then had a few drinks from the sippy cup. That still felt a little embarrassing, but he didn't act like it was out of the ordinary for a grown woman to drink from a child's cup.

She studied him, taking him in. "You look tired. You should get some sleep." She looked carefully around. "Did you sleep in that armchair all night? That doesn't look comfortable."

He grimaced. "It's not. But there is only one bed and I needed to check on you in the night. The sofa's not much comfier anyway."

"It's morning?" He'd sat in that chair all night just to care for her? When had anyone ever done something so selfless for her? And here she was complaining over him shining a light in her eyes.

What a selfish brat she was being.

"You stayed up all night to look after me? You didn't have to do that."

He frowned slightly. "You have a concussion, Ellie. You've been vomiting. You need to see a doctor." He sighed. "Unfortunately, snow's still coming down. Once it eases up, I'll go check on the state of the road but it could be a few more days until we can safely leave. Afraid I don't know enough about head injuries to ensure I'm doing the right thing."

"Thank you," she told him sincerely. "I've never had someone take care of me before."

He looked surprised. "Surely your parents did when you were ill?"

"Maybe when I was younger." She didn't want him feeling sorry for her. "I feel better now. Why don't you get some sleep? I could sit in the chair while you use the bed."

His eyes widened. "You want to sit in the chair while I sleep?"

"Umm. Yes." Why was that so shocking? She tried to sit, to show him she was fine, and agony shot through her head with a ferocity that stole her breath. She took shallow breaths, trying to control the pain and nausea.

"Easy, little girl." He eased her down on the bed. "Lie back down. Jesus, you are in no condition to be moving around like that. What were you thinking?"

"Sick," she managed to croak out.

He slid a supporting arm around her back, helping her sit even as he grabbed a bowl from the nightstand and held it under her mouth. Her stomach clenched and let go and she found herself vomiting in front of him for the second time in twenty-four hours. Not that there was much to come up except for the water she'd just had. She'd already vomited up her meagre breakfast from yesterday. When she thought her stomach had finally calmed down, she slumped back against him. He laid her down gently and took the bowl into the bathroom. She heard the toilet flush and some water run. He came back with the bowl, setting it on the floor. Then he reached for the sippy cup on the nightstand.

"I can drink out of a glass," she told him dryly.

"That would involve sitting you up and I want you to lie as still as possible." He held the sippy cup up to her mouth. She reached up to grab hold of it and he gave her a firm look. "Stay under the covers and keep warm."

She gulped down some water, a little embarrassed by the fact that she enjoyed him caring for her like this. It felt amazing to have this big man look after her. He didn't even know her. And didn't that say something sad about her life that she'd had more care and attention from a stranger than she ever had from her own family?

"Thank you," she murmured as he pulled the cup away.

"Good girl," he told her warmly. "We need to keep your liquids up. I don't like that you have nothing in your tummy to throw up. Don't want you getting dehydrated. You're such a little thing."

"I'm tougher than I look," she told him. "Really, I am."

He gave her a disbelieving look. "Right. It's still pretty early. Why don't you just close your eyes and go off to sleep."

"You'll be here when I wake up?" Worry bit at her.

"I'll be right here. I promise."

"WHAT STORY DO YOU WANT? I can read you a chapter from *To Kill a Mockingbird* or *One Flew over the Cuckoo's Nest*?"

Bear was looking through the small pile of books in the bookshelf. He'd moved the screen back so she could see him. She'd spent all yesterday sleeping on and off and she was feeling much better. However, today he still wasn't letting her out of bed and since he was very rarely out of her sight, she hadn't had a chance to get up and check whether she could move around on her own.

"There's also *The Adventures of Winnie the Pooh* and a big book filled with fairy tales. What's your favorite fairy tale?"

"I don't know."

"You don't know? What was your favorite story as a kid?"

"I don't know." She couldn't remember being read to much as a child.

"Okay, fairytales it is. We'll start with Beauty and the Beast. Seems apt for our situation."

She rolled her eyes, but smiled with pleasure as he sat in the armchair and started reading. She found herself only half-listening as she watched him. What would it be like with this man as her prince?

That was an idiotic thought. She wasn't after a prince and she wasn't looking to be rescued.

Yeah, because he'd already done that. Rescued her. Taken care of her. What had she done for him? Nothing. Her tummy burned. As soon as she could, she'd find some way to pay him back. When he finished, he set the book aside.

"Another story?" she asked hopefully.

He ran his dark gaze over her. "I need to make us some lunch then you need a nap."

She groaned. "I slept for most of yesterday, and I slept in this morning. I don't need any more sleep."

"You still look tired."

"I'm not. I never sleep this much. I'm pretty certain I could get up now."

He gave her a look under his eyebrows. God, he was sexy. Who knew that listening to a man read to you could be so damn arousing? "Who is in charge?"

She sighed. Damn it. "You are, I guess."

He tapped her nose. "You guess? I am most certainly in charge. And you are staying in bed. You need your sleep."

"I've had heaps of sleep. I feel much better. It's time I got up and did things for myself. Like going to the toilet." Now she could feel herself blushing.

Bear ran his thumb over her cheek. She shivered, hoping he didn't notice the movement. His touch filled her with heat. She longed to pull his arms around her. She wanted to be wrapped up in his warmth, his safety. Her clit throbbed. She had never been this turned on in her life. What if he noticed how wet her panties were the next time he took her to the bathroom? She'd need to keep him from seeing. "Hey now, there's no reason to be embarrassed. You're sick."

"Yeah...but...it's just so damn embarrassing!"

"Why? You need my help and I'm here to give it. I, for one, am grateful."

That made her open her eyes to gape up at him. "You're grateful that you get to wipe my butt?"

He gave her an exasperated look. "Grateful that I found you when I did. If I hadn't come along you could have gotten hypothermia and died. Having someone help you do things that you can't do for yourself is a small price to pay for being alive, yes?"

"Yeah. I suppose. Still can't help but feel a bit weird about it all."

"Do you remember me telling you that I'm a Daddy Dom?"

"Oh." She thought back. She did have a hazy memory of that. Things were a bit fuzzy from that first day. "Oh God, did I tell you that I wanted a Daddy Dom?"

"You did. Don't worry, you let me down gently when you told me that you weren't looking for a relationship."

"Huh, I said that, did I?" she muttered.

His eyes widened at her statement. "Sorry," she said quickly. What the hell was she thinking? Way to freak him out. "Forget I said that."

He studied her. "You said you liked to read about BDSM."

"Yeah, I do. But I also like to read about murder-mysteries and I really have no desire to meet a murderer."

"Did reading those books turn you on?" he asked bluntly.

"Bear!" she protested. Okay, now she really wanted to find a place to hide and wait for her embarrassment to dissipate. Should only take about fifty years or so.

"Hmm. I'd say that's a definite yes. Have you ever thought about looking for a Dom?"

"You think I'm submissive? Maybe I'd be the Domme?" Yeah, right.

He just gave her a look. "Baby, you are definitely submissive."

She cleared her throat. "Umm, no. I mean, maybe I've thought about it but it's not something I'm going to do. Well, perhaps in the future, but I'm not looking for a relationship. I just got my freedom. I want to be alone for a while."

"That's an interesting statement. Your freedom? That implies you were a prisoner, who was holding you captive?" There was a dark note to his voice and she swallowed, feeling a little nervous around him.

"What? No one. Sorry, I was being overly dramatic, I guess. Don't listen to me."

"Lying isn't allowed, you know."

"W-what?"

"Dishonesty isn't good in any relationship, but between a Dom and his submissive, communication is key. No lying."

"Oh, right, but I just told you..."

"I know what you told me," he said calmly. "I also know you're a submissive. One who makes bad decisions and puts herself at risk."

Okay, she wanted to argue that. Except a bad decision was how she'd ended up lying in this bed.

"I've never thought of myself as a submissive." Except hadn't she done what her parents had told her to for years, hadn't she? "I don't want to end up in a relationship with someone who's going to use me. Who will walk all over me."

His gaze narrowed. "A good Dominant would never use you. He'd put you first."

"Yeah? I haven't experienced that much. How would I know a good Dom from a bad one who would just take advantage of me?"

He watched her thoughtfully. Why the hell was she having this conversation with a man she'd just met? But she was curious about this stuff. And it wasn't like she had anyone to ask.

"See, this is why it's best that I be on my own," she told him, managing a small smile.

"I don't know about that. You clearly need a keeper."

"I do not!" She glared at him.

Strangely, he just smiled at her. "You're cute when you're mad."

"That's pretty condescending. I'm not cute."

He leaned forward and tapped her nose. "Definitely cute. You know, we're stuck here for a few days. I will be taking care of you.

Would you like me to show you what having a Daddy Dom would be like while we're here?"

Okay, she'd just fallen down the rabbit hole.

"Ellie, you can totally say no. In fact, maybe it would be a good thing to say no. This will probably be a disaster. Can't quite believe I offered..." he trailed off with a frown. "But I want you to know what to look for in a Dom, I don't want you getting taken advantage of."

"I can take care of myself, you know." Maybe. She wasn't really sure.

He gave her a skeptical look and she caved. "All right, maybe I can't. I live in this world in my head where I'm a kickass bitch, instead I'm a mousy little coward who lets people take advantage of her."

"I don't want to hear you talking about yourself like that. You are not mousy or a coward." His voice had grown low. Stern. "That's rule three."

Her nipples hardened. Why did that tone of voice turn her on? "Rule three?"

"Rule one is no getting up without my help. Rule two is no lying. Rule three is no talking down about yourself."

She licked her lips. "Considering I haven't agreed to anything; I don't think I should have rules."

He grinned. "But you so clearly need them."

"Not sure I like this image you have of me as a wimp."

He leaned forward. "I don't see you as a wimp, honey. Not at all. I see you as someone who needs a bit of guidance. You're a little reckless with your safety. You could use someone to watch over you." He shook his head, rubbing at the back of his neck. "Look, don't worry about any of this. Forget I said it, okay?"

He stood up. "No, wait." She reached out and grabbed his arm.

He stilled and gave her a disapproving look. Not because she had touched him, she knew, but because she'd pulled her arm out from under the blankets. Jeez, he was overprotective.

And damned if she didn't love that.

Here was this gorgeous hunk of a man, who could probably have any woman he wanted, and he was fussing over her. Why, she wasn't exactly sure. She wasn't anything special.

"What about sex?" She blushed bright red, unable to believe she'd said that. And did she want sex to be part of the deal? Damned if she knew.

He didn't take offence. Instead he gave her an incredulous look. "You can't even pee by yourself, how do you expect to have sex?"

"I just...I don't know. I don't really know much about sex at all." Crap. Why had she told him that? Men liked experienced women, didn't they?

He was silent for a moment. "Have you had sex before, Ellie?"

"Umm...well...no." She kept her gaze averted from him, not wanting to see his reaction.

"Look at me," he demanded.

No way.

"Ellie. Eyes on me. Now."

She turned her gaze to him.

"Honey, there is nothing wrong with being a virgin."

"Isn't there? Don't men like women with experience? Who know what they're doing?" she asked.

"Maybe some do. Experience can be good. So can innocence. Ellie, are you attracted to me?"

"I can't believe you are asking me that," she groaned. "Can we just forget I said any of this?"

"Nope. Are you attracted to me?"

When she still didn't say anything, he sat and gave her a stern look. "Daddy expects an answer when he asks a question, little girl."

Those words were like a trigger inside her. She wanted to answer him, please him. It scared her how much she wanted that.

He reached out and cupped hold of her chin, lifting her face. "You can tell me anything, little one. Daddy will always listen."

"Yes, I'm attracted to you," she whispered.

"Good. I'm attracted to you too."

"You are?" She stared at him in shock.

"That's such a surprise?"

Well, yeah, frankly it was.

"But..." he said.

Here it came, the dreaded but.

"You are not up to anything much at the moment, and I'm not going to risk your health. I also don't want to take advantage of you. So, nothing is going to happen right now. Later, if you want it to, we'll see."

So, it wasn't an absolute no. And he said he was attracted to her.

"All right," she agreed.

"Good."

"Is that why you offered to do this? Because you're attracted to me? I mean, I'm guessing it's not that you've fallen instantly in love with me."

He grinned. "No instant love."

"I don't...I'm not looking for anything permanent." She didn't want to go into this without making that clear.

"Neither am I," he said simply. "Like I said, this lasts for as long as we are here."

That should have been a relief. For some reason, it wasn't. "I feel like agreeing to this wouldn't be fair to you. What would you be getting in return?"

He just stared at her, studied her like she was some weird species of bug he'd just discovered. "Not fair to me?"

The balance wasn't even. It felt wrong just to take from him without giving him something in return.

"Umm, yeah. You've been so amazing, rescuing me, taking care of me. If I can pay you back in any way, I will. I don't have any money, I'm afraid, so I can't offer to pay you.... but once I have a job..." the thunderous look on his face made her trail off. She licked her lips nervously. She wasn't scared of him exactly, but he did look rather intimidating right now.

"You, umm, look a little mad."

"Do I? Maybe it's just because you offered to pay me for taking care of you. Do you think I work for you?"

"No. I didn't mean it like that." Misery swamped her. "I'm sorry. I'm not very good at talking to people. I don't have friends anymore. My last boyfriend was when I was seventeen. I'm pretty damn pathetic really. Maybe you could do me a huge favor and forget we ever had this conversation."

NOPE. That wasn't happening. He especially wasn't going to forget the part where she'd said she was attracted to him. His cock was hard and pressing against his zipper. How had she not had a boyfriend since high school? He had her pegged at around twenty-three. Were the men in Florida blind? She was gorgeous. Sweet. And submissive. How had some Dom not snapped her up? She should be completely and utterly cherished for the gift she was.

Someone else's loss is your gain.

Nope. He couldn't think like that. Neither of them was looking for something permanent. He'd only known her a short time. He felt protective of her because she was so helpless, that was all. He couldn't stand the idea of her being taken advantage of and he couldn't stand to think about that happening again.

How had she thought he wouldn't get anything out of this?

Because she doesn't understand, dumb ass.

He sat back in the armchair. "Your objection to doing this is that you think I won't get anything in return?"

"I-I guess so. I mean, I'm also a little nervous. I don't know how I'll react to any of this."

He nodded. "That's totally understandable. I get that. Which is why you'd have a safe word."

"A safe word? I'd need that?" She looked alarmed.

"Easy, honey," he told her with a smile. "Not because I'm going to strip you naked, tie you up and spank you. You're definitely not up to that. And I would never risk your health, understand?"

"Yes. So why would I need a safe word?"

"Because this is new to you and you might find it overwhelming and need some way to make it stop. Littles can easily get out of their depths. It's a big scary world sometimes when you don't have a daddy to guide and protect you."

Tears filled her eyes. "You know exactly what to say, don't you?"

"I'm being sincere, little girl. I haven't had many Littles in my life. Most women are scared by my size. And my sometimes abrupt manner."

"I'm not."

He raised an eyebrow. "You lying to me, little girl? Remember the rules."

Her eyes widened. "What happens if I break the rules?"

"Then you get punished."

"H-how?"

"You don't remember our talk about spankings?" She had been half-asleep at the time.

She just stared up at him, looking shocked. "You'd spank me?"

"Not while you're ill. But you won't be sick forever, now, will you?" he said in a low voice.

She bit at her lip.

"Besides, I'm betting I could think of some punishment other than a spanking. Not that you're up to writing lines or standing in the corner."

He heard her small gasp. "Those are normal punishments for a Little?"

"Yes. And not just for Littles. Of course, not every daddy/little girl relationship is the same. So, you can't treat it as a one size fits all, understand?"

"Yes."

He wanted to insist that she address him as Daddy, but he was well aware she hadn't agreed to be his temporary little girl.

Yet.

"I wasn't lying, though," she said earnestly.

"You shied away from me that first day."

"God, I can't believe that was just the day before yesterday. It feels like much longer. I just got a fright. I think that's normal. But I'm really not scared of you. You've taken better care of me than anyone ever has before."

He ran his hand over his face tiredly. "You really do need a keeper."

"Why?"

"Because you're going to get in trouble going around trusting people so easily."

"But you said I could trust you," she pointed out.

"Yes...but..." Okay, what was he arguing about? He wanted her trust. He just didn't want her to trust anyone else. Which was pretty damn selfish of him, wasn't it?

"Okay, forget about that. I want to make a couple of things clear. No matter what you decide, you don't owe me anything. You are not paying me." He scowled at her.

"Maybe I could do something around here to help out then?"

There was no way he wanted her doing chores out of a sense of obligation. He got that she was feeling better and that's why she was pushing him. But she still needed to take things easy.

"I don't need you to do anything to pay me back."

"You really don't want me to do anything to help out?" She looked slightly anxious about that.

"I don't. Listen carefully, because this is very important. I am not offering this just for your benefit. Yes, I want to show you what it's like to have a Daddy Dom because I worry you might be taken advantage of. However, I am not doing this because I'm selfless. The reason I like being a Daddy Dom is because I have a huge desire to be needed. To take care of someone. Caregiver, protector, disciplinarian, monster destroyer."

She smiled.

"So, don't think I'm doing this just for you, I'm not. But it is entirely up to you whether you take up the offer."

"I can say my safe word at any time?"

"Yes, without any fear that I'll walk away or get upset or mad. That I promise."

"And I'll call you Daddy. And I'll do what you say, within reason—"

"Within reason?"

"Well, if you order me to run naked through the snow, I'm not going to do that."

He snorted. "All right, within reason. Although if I was the kind of man to do that, I'd expect you to get out of my company as soon as possible."

"And you'll show me what it's like to have a Daddy Dom. You'll take care of me. Like I'm really your sub, your Little."

"Yes. Would you like some time to think about it?" He really didn't think she was going to go for it. Why would she? She barely knew him.

"I don't need any time. I agree...D-daddy."

SHE COULDN'T BELIEVE she'd just said yes.

What was she thinking?

And yet, when was she going to get an offer like this again? There wasn't much chance of her meeting another Daddy Dom. And pretty much a zero chance of meeting one who was willing to show her what it would be like to let her Little side free in a safe place without asking for any kind of commitment.

So yeah, she'd said yes. Only what happened now?

Her tummy danced with nerves. This was crazy. So unlike anything she'd done before.

He looked surprised but then his gaze filled with warmth. "All right. What would you like to use as your safe word?"

"Umm." What the hell? She had no idea.

"Something a little unusual but short enough you can say it easily. Of course, you can always just tell me you need a breather or to stop for a while."

"How about Hawaii?" she asked.

"Hawaii, that works. Any reason why?"

"I've always wanted to visit," she said a little wistfully.

"Feels like a world away from winter in Montana," he said with a smile. "Okay, so communication between a Dom and his sub is key. You talk everything out first so there are no surprises. No misunderstandings. Or less of them, anyway. Guess there are always going to be misunderstandings in relationships. You get it all in writing. Always, always have a contract. Okay?"

"Yes, okay." She was starting to feel a bit intimidated by all of this. "We don't have one."

"We should." He frowned as though thinking that over. "But we're not doing anything hardcore. I'm not into it and you're not up to it."

"I trust you."

"Another thing. Don't trust so easy. Don't ever play unless there are people around who know what's going on and will keep an eye on you."

"I don't want to be tied to a cross and have some stranger take a crop to my ass. I don't think I'll ever be going to a club or anything."

He nodded. "You already have three rules. The next rule is that I am fully in charge of safety. You feel unsafe. You get into trouble, you call me. You put yourself in a dangerous situation, you'll be in trouble once I'm sure you're safe."

Her bottom tingled. Although it was difficult to believe that she could get up to much trouble stuck here in this cabin. And this was only a temporary arrangement.

"I am in charge of health. Which means I'll be watching you closely for any signs of my baby feeling unwell. I will be making certain you eat right. If you start to feel ill, you tell me immediately so I can take proper care of you. I expect you to tell me if you feel nauseous, are in pain, need something from me, understand?"

"Yes."

"As well as the rules you already have, I set bedtimes. I set chores. I set any sort of routines. Not something you need to worry about since you're not well enough for chores. And well, routine has kind of gone out the window. But still, that's what you can expect. Questions?"

"I don't think so. Only, what will you do if I break the rules? Since you can't spank me?"

"Like I said, I'll find something. Or I'll just keep track for one hell of a spanking at the end."

"Something to look forward to," she muttered. Then blushed. She couldn't believe she'd just said that. She didn't actually want him to spank her, did she?

"Oh, believe me, it won't be."

～

HE WARMED up some soup for their lunch.

He could hardly believe she'd agreed to be his little girl while she was here. He was determined to make it a good experience. Although he wouldn't hesitate to punish her, especially if she put her health at risk.

How he'd do that would be a challenge. Couldn't give her an early bedtime when she was stuck in bed anyway. She didn't have anything he could take off her. He couldn't take away screen time.

Some Doms would withdraw their attention from a naughty sub. Not him. Looked like he might actually need to start keeping a notebook or something.

When he decided the soup was warm enough, he poured some into a bowl and grabbed a spoon and a towel.

"Okay, little girl. Your soup is ready."

She didn't open her eyes. She looked paler than she had before. Idiot. She'd gone too long without pain killers and she wasn't good at asking for what she needed. He looked over at the sippy cup. She hadn't had any more to drink either.

Yeah, some daddy he was.

He moved back over to where she lay. "Not feeling well, are you, baby?"

"Not really," she whispered back. "Can I have some pain killers?"

"I'd rather you had something in your tummy first," he told her. "Don't want you getting sick again. Or dehydrated."

She looked over at him then down at the soup. "Don't think I can. Head hurts. So much."

That worried him. He'd thought her head would be feeling better. But then he was no doctor. "All right." He grabbed a couple of painkillers and helped her take them. Then he softly massaged the back of her neck until that pinched look left her face.

"How are you feeling?" he finally asked.

"A little better," she told him, opening her eyes to look up at him. "But I still don't feel like eating."

"All right. But you have to drink some water for me. You can have soup later." He was worried about her getting dehydrated. It had been a while since he'd taken her to the toilet.

He held up the sippy cup. Amazingly, she didn't reach for it. But she only took a few sips.

"Baby girl, do you need Daddy to take you to the potty?"

The red on her cheeks deepened. "No."

"No, what?"

She looked confused for a moment then her face cleared and she gave him a shy look. "No, Daddy."

"All right, but I expect you to tell me as soon as you need to go, all right? It's not good for you to hold on just because you're embarrassed."

"Somehow, I don't think I'll ever not be embarrassed about being asked that," she said dryly.

He just grinned.

4

He heard her murmur something and turned away from the fireplace to walk over to the bed. It was still early, but he wasn't one to sleep in. Her eyes fluttered open and she looked blurrily up at him.

He settled himself next to her on the bed and carefully maneuvered her so she was sitting up slightly, resting back against his arm. Then he held the sippy cup to her lips.

"Bear?"

"What do you call me?" His voice was rougher than he would have liked, worry for her making him a bit short on patience.

"Sorry, Daddy. What ya doing?"

"Helping you drink."

"Oh okay." She took a few sips.

"Have some more," he encouraged. "You've drunk hardly anything and your pee has been bright yellow."

"I know I should be embarrassed that you know that, but I'm just too tired."

"I told you nothing is embarrassing between a daddy and his

little girl. Now, drink some more or I'm going to have to get strict with you."

"What? Why? I'm a good girl, Daddy."

She was slipping into Little space. Hmm, was it his voice that did it? Or his words? For some Littles it was what they wore or did. Others it was more verbal.

"Of course, you're a good girl. You're Daddy's very good girl. Which is why you're going to do what Daddy says and drink down all this yummy water."

She wrinkled her nose.

"If you don't drink it then Daddy will have to punish his naughty girl, won't he? And when you're feeling better, I'd bet you'd much rather play than be taken over my knee for a spanking."

"Never had a spanking."

"Your parents never spanked you?"

"No. If they were mad at me, they just ignored me."

Jesus. He'd been expecting her to say she had to go to time out or write lines or she'd had something taken away. What sort of parents took away their attention?

"Well, I'll never ignore you as punishment, baby girl. I'll tip you up over my knee, pull those cute panties down until your bottom is revealed then I'll start smacking that little ass until it turns pink then crimson. Then when you're crying out, your feet kicking, I'll move my hand to the top of your thighs. If what you did was really bad, like risking your health or safety, I might make you stand in the corner with that bright red bottom on display. Then after a while I'd have you come back and lean over the back of the chair or the bed and I'd get my paddle or belt and give you some extras to remind you of who you belong to and what my expectations are of you. So, you'll know that next time you put yourself at risk that there is someone who lo—," he cut himself off, "who cares about you and is holding you accountable."

Her eyes were wide as she stared at him. *Good one. Way to terrify her.*

"So, you won't stop talking to me for a week?"

"How am I going to take care of my girl if we're not communicating? And once a punishment is given then that's it. All is forgiven."

"Really?" She looked at him in amazement as though that was a completely foreign concept. Given her upbringing he guessed it was.

"Yes," he told her firmly. "Unless I've told you that you've earned yourself more punishment. But that would be rare."

"I like your way better than my parents'."

Yeah. So, did he.

"Good, so drink your water like a good girl."

She started to suck it down slowly but he didn't hurry her. She was doing what he'd told her to. She drank most of it before turning her head away with a sigh.

"No more, Daddy."

"Good girl. I'm very pleased with you."

She smiled up at him.

ELLIE WAS FEELING REALLY GRUMPY. She wasn't sure why. She wasn't a grumpy person by nature. Most of the time she was pretty happy. But as she sat up in bed and looked down at the porridge Bear had made for her breakfast, she felt the urge to throw it away and pout.

She took a deep breath and let it out slowly.

"Something wrong, baby girl?"

"No."

For some reason his patient tone just made her even grumpier.

"You've got a face like a thundercloud and you're not eating your porridge."

"Don't like it." She curled up her lip. What was wrong with her? She loved porridge normally. And she had no reason to be so awful to Bear who had been nothing but kind to her. God, he'd spent the last few days trying to coax her into eating and drinking, carting her back and forth to the bathroom and giving her medicine.

Maybe that's why she was upset. She wasn't used to someone doing everything for her. He still wouldn't let her out of bed and she wasn't allowed to go to the bathroom on her own yet.

She just felt ridiculously out of sorts.

"I could try and find something else to eat."

"No."

"No, thank you," he said. Her insides trembled at the stern note in his voice. He came over to the bed, took the porridge and put it on the nightstand and sat facing her on the bed.

"So, you want to tell me what's going on? This isn't like you. Why are you being so snappy and rude?"

To her horror, and his, she guessed by the look on his face, she burst into tears. He immediately pulled her into his arms, rocking her gently. Which just made her cry all the more.

"How can you be so nice to me when I'm being so horrid?" she wailed. "I'm an awful, terrible person."

"No, you're not. And I don't like hearing you say such mean things about yourself."

"But it's true, I'm being so awful to you and you've been nothing but nice to me. You've taken care of me, done everything for me and I...I..."

"Yes?"

"I just feel so grouchy. I don't know what's wrong with me."

"Shh. Shh. Let it all out." He rubbed his hand up and down her back soothingly until she'd quieted down. Then he lay her back down and got up. She had to fight the urge to call him back to her. It was ridiculous, he only went as far as the bathroom and he quickly returned with a roll of toilet paper in his hand.

"Going to run out of this stuff soon if we're not careful," he told her with a grin as he wiped her face then held it to her nose. "Blow."

"I can do that myself." Sheesh, she might have been ill but she wasn't an invalid.

He gave her a stern look. "Put your hand down, little one, and blow."

She blew her nose and he wiped her clean, turning to throw the used tissue in a trash can. Then he turned back and gave her a stern look. "Now. I know you're feeling better. Might be you're itching to get out of that bed and that's what's got you so out of sorts."

"Maybe," she whispered. "I guess."

"You guess?" He looked thoughtful. "You know, I've been thinking about how much you've slept these past few days. Had me really worried about you."

"I...I'm sorry?" Was he upset about that? But he was the one who was keeping her in bed, so it couldn't be that.

"Nothing to be sorry about. I'm just wondering if there was more to it than your head injury."

And now she felt even worse. "I'm sorry, Bear. I really am a horrible, selfish person for treating you like this when you've been nothing but kind."

"That's one," he told her.

"What?"

"I've given you plenty of warnings about not putting yourself down. So that's one spanking you've earned."

Her eyes widened and she gaped at him. "You...you're going to spank me?"

"Not right now. I believe a spanking should be given when earned, but you're not well enough."

And he'd never do anything to endanger her health because he was an honorable guy. She sniffled.

"Baby girl, you've been through a lot. And nobody expects you to be perfect all the time. If your attitude becomes too much, if it's disrespectful, then I will take you in hand."

Was there something wrong with her that she liked when he got all bossy and dominant? He studied her for a moment. "I know you're feeling better, but you're not getting out of that bed until I'm assured of your health, understand?"

She wasn't happy about that but she nodded. At least it no longer hurt to move her head. She really was feeling a lot better.

"Words," he said in a warning voice.

"Yes, Daddy."

He ran his hand through his hair. "I'm sorry I don't have much to offer you for entertainment. Hopefully we'll be able to leave here soon. Do you want me to read to you again?"

Hurt filled her. It was stupid. She barely knew him. They had a temporary little girl/daddy dynamic going on but that was all it was. Temporary. And yet she felt ridiculously upset because he wanted to leave. Once they got out of here, they'd each have to go their separate ways.

And isn't that what you want? To get on with your life? Alone. Not answering to anyone? Having no demands on you? And it wasn't like he'd ever promised her more so she had no right to feel so out of sorts with him.

But she did.

"Ellie? You listening to me?" There was a deep rumble to his voice which indicated he was about to put his foot down. She was learning the different sides to him. He was far more dominant than he might seem on the surface. Mostly he had that tall, dark and silent thing going on. But once he'd agreed to be her temporary daddy his dominant side came out more.

And when he thought she needed something for her health, he didn't hesitate to lay down the law.

Fuck, that was a big turn on.

"Sorry, Daddy. Daydreaming."

He tapped her nose. "When Daddy is talking to you, I want you to pay attention, understand?"

"Yes, Daddy," she answered dutifully.

"Where'd you live in Florida?" he asked as he picked up the porridge. No doubt it was cold by now.

He went to the stovetop and poured it back into the pot, reheating it. He sat in the armchair beside her and spooning some up, blew on it. Then he brought it to his lips as though to test the temperature. He pressed a spoonful against her mouth. She thought about arguing, but her tummy was grumbling.

She took the mouthful he offered.

"Miami," she said.

"Cool place. What are you doing in Montana?"

She smiled at him. "My aunt, well, my great-aunt she left me her house, not too far from here, I think. I'm not really good with directions."

He looked a bit surprised. "So, you came up here to take a look at the house?"

"No, I came up here to live."

He frowned. "Without doing any research into the weather? You don't have any winter clothing with you. Everything you packed was summer stuff. Is a moving company bringing every-thing else?"

She didn't really want to explain it all. But she knew it made no sense for her to have one piece of luggage with her.

"And why were you driving around with a near empty tank? Without snow tires on your car? Why didn't you wait until the end of winter to move up here?"

She sighed. "I didn't know I'd inherited the house until a week or so ago and I've never been here before. I know I wasn't well prepared, but I didn't have the money to buy a whole lot of stuff."

He looked slightly alarmed at that.

"It's okay, apparently my aunt left a trust fund too. I just have to meet with the lawyer to pick the keys up, along with any paperwork."

He just fed her more porridge. She swallowed. "I'm really sorry for the way I behaved just before."

He waved that off. "I know you are, baby girl. How long did the trip from Miami to here take you?"

"Umm, about four days."

"Four days?" He stared at her. "That's a huge trip. You must have been traveling ten-hour days."

"Yeah, more if you add in stops." She blushed. "I don't have a GPS and I got lost a few times when trying to use my phone to navigate. Like I said, I don't have the best sense of direction."

"That wasn't a smart idea, little girl. No wonder you were sleeping so much. You were exhausted! You could have fallen asleep at the wheel, had an accident and killed yourself or someone else."

"I know," she whispered. "But I didn't have much choice. I left home with just a few hundred dollars and I spent most of that on gas. I couldn't afford too many nights in motels along the way. So, I drove as much as I could. I thought I had enough gas to make it to my aunt's house. I've never driven in snow and when I came around that corner to find the tree in the path, well, I instinctively slammed on the brakes."

She shrugged. "Rest is history, right?"

"No, it is not history. Had you been mine, I can tell you that I would not want you driving halfway across the country alone. And if there was no other choice but for that to happen, you'd be restricted to driving for only six hours each day, I'd be mapping out your route, deciding on places for you to stay, and I'd be in constant touch."

It probably should have sounded controlling. Instead, she could only wonder what it would be like to have someone worry about her that much.

"So, you want to tell me who the hell is supposed to be looking after you and failed their job?"

"I-I don't have anyone. Do you think I would have agreed to... to what we're doing if I had a boyfriend?"

"No. I know you don't have a boyfriend. You told me you hadn't had one since high school."

Oh, that's right. Jesus, why had she told him that?

"But what about your parents? Didn't they care? Siblings? Family?"

"I don't have any family left. Not anymore," she said sadly.

"Oh, baby. What happened? Did your parents die?"

"I thought they were going to, but it turns out they were just lying to me all along." She looked up and saw his confused look. "This is a really pathetic story; believe me, you don't want to know."

And she didn't want to tell him. She came off as a naïve idiot who'd fallen for a bunch of lies.

"Oh, I think I do. I'd very much like to know what forced you to leave your home with just a few hundred dollars and drive all the way across the country to a place you've never been before."

She bit at her lip. "I'm feeling a bit tired..."

"What's rule number one, little girl?"

"I'm not allowed to lie. Does that mean I have to tell you everything?"

He sighed, looking reluctant. "No. But I would like to know. It will help me to understand why you put your health and safety at risk like you did. Especially when you're well enough for me to spank you for it."

Her mouth dropped open. "You can't spank me for it!"

OKAY. It might have been going a step too far. After all, she hadn't been his when she'd done that. She wasn't truly his now. But by God, his hands itched to take her over his knee, bare her buttocks and spank her ass for taking such a risk. And he needed to ensure that she never took a risk like that again. So, if spanking her kept her safe in the future, then he was all for it.

"Can't I?" He raised one eyebrow.

She gave him a worried look. "I didn't even know you then. Therefore, I didn't know the rules and can't be held accountable for breaking them."

"But you're mine now." Temporarily anyway. "And you must have known that driving for long hours like that was reckless and dangerous. What kind of Dom would I be if I didn't ensure that didn't happen again?"

Shaky ground, and he should probably back off. But he'd said it now and backing off wasn't really his thing. It didn't set a good precedent.

"Well, tell me," he demanded before she could protest any further.

"It's embarrassing," she whispered.

"Ellie, what did I say about things between a little girl and her daddy?"

"This is different," she insisted. "This isn't a little girl thing."

"Tell me, Ellie. I promise I'm not going to judge."

She studied his face then cleared her throat. "When...when I graduated high school, I had plans to go to college. My parents, they had me when they were older. I think my mom was forty, my dad forty-five. They agreed to pay for college if I went to one close by and lived at home." She shrugged. "I didn't really want to stay home. But I also couldn't pay for college myself. So, I did what they wanted. After a few weeks, I'd made some friends in one of my classes. Back then, I was good at making friends. They asked me to this party."

She paused, licked her lips. "I got home at about three in the morning. I'd texted my parents to say I'd be late, but when I walked in, they were sitting in the living room waiting for me. They told me how much I'd worried and disappointed them. They made me feel so guilty for my behavior that I found myself agreeing to a curfew. Even though I was in college, I was living in their house so I thought that fair. But after a while, it got annoying. I was the only person at college with a curfew. I wanted more. I wanted some fun. So, after that first year, I told them I wanted to move out to live with my friends. I was hoping they'd be supportive."

She paused, looked off into the distance. "That's when Dad had a heart attack."

"Baby, I'm sorry." He grabbed her hand, squeezing it.

"I was so worried about him. My mom seemed so lost, like she didn't know how to take care of him. So, I started doing more and more. They were retired by then and even though they weren't that old they weren't coping. So, I took over doing the grocery shopping, taking my dad to appointments, doing the housework. My schoolwork suffered until eventually I figured I better drop out for a while."

"You had to drop out of college? Couldn't you find someone to take care of them?" He frowned.

She grimaced. "They told me they didn't have the money for that. Finally, my dad seemed to be feeling better. They were going out, doing things. I'd kept in touch with my friends, I decided to go back to college. I'd just re-enrolled when Mom found out she had cancer."

"Jesus, what bad luck."

"Sounds that way, doesn't it?" she said with a bitter smile. "I had to take her to treatments and appointments, only she never wanted me to come in with her. She didn't want to worry me, she said. I was basically doing everything by then. My dad wasn't up to it because of the heart attack and they both needed me."

"Was your mom okay?"

"What? Oh yeah, she was. *Is*. They both are. When I started to question why the treatments were going on so long and if she wanted me to speak to her doctor about a different specialist, she kept telling me that I didn't know what I was talking about. I was a college dropout so what did I know?"

"That wasn't kind." Her parents sounded like horrid people. How could they treat their own daughter like that? And Ellie was such a sweet, loving person.

"Our family was small. My parents were both only children like me so I wasn't used to having family around. All we had was my mom's Aunt Rose. She was a great lady. She'd visit a few times a year, she never had children and my mom was her only niece. She used to travel to exotic places and she'd bring me back these treasures. Most of them my mother threw out, said they were just clutter." She looked down at her hands. "When she died about eight months ago, I was devastated. I never gave much thought about who she left her estate to."

She glanced at him, her eyes blurring with tears. "Turns out she left everything to me in her will and they kept it all from me. I never thought about why they always insisted on getting the mail. But, well, it was so they could keep me ignorant."

"Jesus, why would they do that?"

"To keep me with them. They lied to me. Oh, my dad's heart

attack was real. There was no way to fake that, but it certainly wasn't as bad as he and mom made out. The cancer was completely fabricated. So were my dad's kidney issues, unless they've started doing dialysis in bars now."

"They faked their illnesses to keep you with them?" They'd used her. Taken advantage of her love for them and her innate need to care for and please them.

"Sounds like something out of a soap opera, right? I mean, why take care of yourself or pay someone to do it when you can have your own little slave? And the worst part of it is I never even suspected. Poor, stupid Ellie, she believes every word we say and she'll just keep slaving away, doing whatever we want. I only found out because my dad left his phone in my car after I dropped him off at the hospital. I turned around to take it back to him. Imagine my shock when I saw him walking along the street ahead of me. I followed him. He walked into a bar. I still didn't believe it. I thought maybe something happened to his appointment and he'd had to go to the bar to call me. Stupid, but I didn't want to believe the worst. I followed him inside just in time to see him buy a drink, which by the way he wasn't allowed with his illness."

"What did you do?"

"Well, I didn't confront him then and there. I thought about it. Dreamed of storming over to him and telling him what I thought of him. But I don't like confrontation. So instead, I went home. Like a wimp."

"Careful, little girl," he warned. "You're already in trouble for putting yourself down." He hated that she thought so badly of herself.

She gave him an incredulous look. "I don't think it can be considered putting myself down when it's the truth."

"It is *not* the truth."

"Damn it, Bear. You don't understand what a doormat I was.

They used me. For years! And I never once questioned it. I just went along with everything like a stupid, foolish child."

"Enough." He leaned over and grabbed her around the waist, pulling her gently onto his lap. He tucked her in against his chest as she started to cry. She kind of melted into him. Not for the first time, he'd wondered if she was a bit starved for touch, affection. Now he was almost certain.

"Enough," he repeated more gently. "None of this was your fault. It was all on them, baby. All them."

"I c-called their doctor. I pretended to be worried over my father's kidney treatments. I could hear from the silence on the other end that the doctor had no idea what I was talking about. I thought he'd tell me he couldn't say anything because of confidentiality agreements. I'd known Doctor Steward all my life. He kind of cleared his throat then told me that my parents were two of the healthiest people he knew. That my dad's heart attack had been mild and he'd been lucky but as long as he didn't drink too much and ate healthy, he'd be fine."

She placed her hand on his wide, warm chest, soaking in his comfort. Even though she knew this really was her fault.

Naïve, stupid idiot.

He ran his hand up and down her back, crooning to her under his breath. "So, you left?"

She nodded, taking in a shuddering breath. She wiped at her cheeks. "Not right away. I didn't have any money or anywhere to go. So, I pretended everything was okay, while I squirreled away money. Whenever I was alone in the house, I went through any paperwork I could find. One day, I found the letter from the lawyer about Aunt Rose's estate. It was like a Godsend. I packed a suitcase, filled it with everything I wanted to take which wasn't much. I thought they were hard up for money so I'd been wearing the same clothes I had since high school. Just as well I hadn't put on any weight. Thankfully, my aunt had bought me a secondhand car for my graduation present."

He kept rubbing his hand up and down her back.

"My parents walked in as I was coming down the stairs. They both wanted to know what was going on, why I had a suitcase. I told them I was leaving. That I knew they'd been lying to me and I was no longer staying here to wait on them hand and foot. They were furious. They threatened that if I walked out that door then I was no longer their daughter. They'd cut me off entirely."

"Oh, baby. That had to hurt."

"I told them I didn't care, that parents who loved their child wouldn't treat them like they'd treated me. They yelled horrible things at me, how I'd never amount to anything, how I'd come crawling back when I realized that I couldn't make it on my own."

His heart hurt for her. "None of that is true. You did a brave thing driving halfway across the country to a place you'd never been to. My poor little girl. It's okay. You're not on your own now. I'm here."

"It felt so freeing to leave. Sure, it was scary. I didn't know what would happen when I got here. I don't know how much is in the trust my aunt left me. I'll probably need to find a job. I don't know what state my aunt's house is in."

"No wonder you were so scared." The bravery it had taken her to do what she had astounded him. Even as he couldn't help but think of all the things that could have gone wrong.

"I've lived all my life by someone else's rules. Done what others wanted of me. I feel like for the first time I get to be me. To be on my own."

Guilt filled him. Because now she was living by his rules. But it was only temporary. Once they left this cabin, it all ended and she could get on with her life. A knot formed in his gut and he realized there had been a kernel of hope inside him that they might be able to take this beyond these few days. But this sort of relationship would be too constrictive long-term for someone who'd just found their wings and wanted to fly.

He kissed the top of her head. So, he'd shelter her while she was here and then let her go when this had to end. Sounded like she'd spent years in virtual slavery and even though being with him wouldn't be like that, she'd be restricted all the same.

And this was why it was a bad idea to hope. He should have remembered that.

"Is your aunt's house in an isolated area or a town?" he asked her, trying to distract himself from his thoughts.

"Umm, I have the address in my bag. I think it's in a small town, Russell?"

"Russell? That's about an hour from here."

He set her back on the bed, tucking her under the covers again. She gave him a slightly exasperated look but didn't say anything. Okay, so it was nice and toasty in the cabin and she was obviously feeling better. But he still intended to watch her.

He grabbed her handbag and handed it to her. She pulled out a document and gave it to him.

"Do you know Russell at all?" she asked.

"Don't go there much. It's not the closest town to us and you were headed in a strange direction. You must have gotten turned around somewhere. You say the GPS on your phone led you to here?"

"Ah, well, my phone kind of died several hours before you found me," she admitted.

He gave her a look and she shifted around a little. "You're not gonna spank me for that, are you?"

"Little girl, I understand why you traveled halfway across the country with no luggage and little sleep, I don't like it but I get it. But not having your phone charged?" He clenched his hands into fists. "Do you know what could have happened to you?"

"What? Something worse than crashing into a tree, getting a concussion and nearly freezing to death?"

He growled at her. Actually growled.

"I'm beginning to see why your nickname is Bear."

He just gave her a look.

"Want to tell me what your real name is?"

No, he did not.

"You know, I kind of see what happened as a good thing."

"A good thing?"

"Well, if it hadn't happened, I wouldn't have met you." She tilted her head back to smile up at him and he couldn't stop himself.

"You'd find something good in anything, wouldn't you?" he murmured. He leaned in. He shouldn't. He knew that one kiss wasn't going to be enough. And she wasn't up to anything more. But then she licked her lips, her eyes filled with arousal.

He was gone.

He brushed his lips against hers, giving her a chance to push back. To tell him no. But her lips met his eagerly, her body pressing up to meet his. He ran his tongue over the seam of her lips.

"Tell me if you don't want this. Tell me no and I'll back off. Remember, if any of this gets too much or isn't what you want, you just need to say." He didn't want her to ever think he was like her parents.

She reached up and with one hand touched his cheek. "Bear, I want this. I want you. Please kiss me."

"I don't want to take advantage of you." He sat on the mattress, facing her. "I don't want you to think I'm trying to control you."

She rolled her eyes. "Bear, out of everyone I've known in my life, you are the least likely person to take advantage of me. You're so careful, all the time. Like you're worried I'll break or something. I'm not weak or fragile. Just a naïve idiot."

"Three," he growled at her warningly.

"Three? What happened to two?"

"Two was not keeping an eye on the weather and driving into a storm without enough gas or a charged-up phone. Can't punish you for making that trip, when I know you had little choice. But you should have taken more care. Three is for the same reason you earned your first spanking. Talking down about yourself. Once you're feeling better, you're not going to be able to sit comfortably for a while."

Funny he always thought he wouldn't get involved with someone else because he couldn't trust them. But he didn't have any issues trusting her. She was so different from Maria. She didn't have a deceptive bone in her body.

"I want you to know you don't have to say yes to anything just because I'm in a position of authority. Ultimately, you're always in charge. You have your safe word. It stops everything."

She raised her eyebrows. "Even if we were in the middle of..." a blush covered her cheeks.

He ran a finger down her cheek. "No matter what. But when it comes to a punishment that you've earned, remember if you use it then be prepared to pay the price in another way. And I'd only expect you to use it if you truly needed to. It's not a *get out of jail free* card. But yes, you can use it even if we were having sex."

Shit. He couldn't get the idea of stripping her naked and licking her all over out of his head. He wanted to know what she tasted like, wanted to know what noises she made as she came.

She's still weak and recovering, asshole. Plus, she's a virgin. Her first time should be special.

But he still couldn't stop himself from leaning in and kissing her. He was gentle at first. Lips only. But then her mouth parted beneath his and he swept his tongue inside. Heat flooded him. He needed more. Wanted everything. He forced himself to pull back. His breath was fast, ragged.

"That was amazing." She smiled up at him.

Jesus, she was sweet.

"It was," he said gruffly. Fuck, he needed some space. He ran his finger down her cheek then gave her another kiss on the forehead. "Rest. I need to go get some wood." Maybe stepping out into the cool temperatures would work like a cold shower at dousing his arousal.

Maybe.

5

"Put that foot back in the bed," Bear commanded, from where he stood at the counter, drying some dishes. He didn't even look back. Did the man have eyes in the back of his head?

She poked her tongue out at him, but she put the foot she had been creeping out of bed back under the covers.

"I saw that too," he told her. Finally, he turned around to look at her, drying his hands on a towel.

"I wasn't doing anything, Daddy," she said innocently.

He lowered his chin and looked at her sternly from under his eyebrows. He crossed his arms over his wide chest, the towel still held in one hand as he leaned back against the counter.

She heaved a big sigh. "Fine, I'm just bored. I'm tired of being stuck in this bed." It was day four and she'd had enough. "I feel much better."

He gave her a nod. "All right, I'll let you get out of bed."

She clapped her hands excitedly. But she should have known there was going to be a 'but'. There was always a 'but'.

"But you will stay on the sofa." He pointed over at the sofa.

She guessed it was as much as she was going to get out of him. Still she didn't care. She would do anything to get out of this bed. He turned back towards the counter to put the dishes he'd been drying away.

She climbed out of bed before he could change his mind and headed to the sofa. He looked over at her with a frown on his face.

"See, I'm fine. No dizzy spells. I didn't injure myself. There is nothing wrong with me."

He crooked a finger at her and she moved closer to him. He wrapped one arm around her, pulling her so she was flush against him.

"What was the rule about getting out of bed?"

She sighed. "You're being way too overprotective."

"What was the rule?"

"Not to get out of bed without you."

His hand cradled her head against his chest and gave her a couple of sharp smacks to the ass.

"Hey, ouch! What was that for?" She gaped up at him.

He drew her back, giving her a stern look. "That was just a small reminder that you're not to break Daddy's rules for you."

She rubbed at her bottom. Okay, those smacks didn't really hurt. In fact, her body was kind of lit on fire, wanting more. But she thought she should make a token protest. Daddy grabbed hold of her hands. "No rubbing."

"You've got lots of mean rules, Daddy."

"I know, Daddy is just a big old meanie. But you know how to avoid being spanked, don't you?"

"I suppose so," she muttered.

He led her over to the sofa. "Sit."

She sat. She didn't want to push him too far. And really, she was getting what she wanted. He placed a blanket that had been lying over the end of the sofa over her bare legs. Then without a word, he went searching in the chest where the board games were kept.

When he returned, he held a pad and a box of colored pencils in his hand. He placed them on her lap.

"What is this?" she asked.

"I thought you could draw me a picture."

"Of what?"

"Of anything you like, baby. I'll get you a drink and a snack."

He moved away from her without another word. Adult Ellie warred with her Little side. She hadn't drawn a picture since she was in kindergarten. But what else did she have to do?

She started drawing. She barely noticed him putting the snack and drink, still in the sippy cup, on the coffee table in front of her.

"Eat your snack, baby girl," he said to her.

She glanced up and over to see a couple of chocolate chip cookies on a plate.

"Yummy!" She reached over and grabbed one.

Bear sat on the other end of the sofa with a book in hand. "Don't expect it all the time. I know little girls tend to have a sweet tooth, but I don't want you getting holes in your teeth."

She was too busy munching on the cookie and drawing to pay attention. When she finished her masterpiece, she held it up to him.

"What do you think, Daddy?"

He looked over at her then studied the picture. "Looks great, baby girl. Is that you?" He pointed at the figure dressed in a yellow dress with ruffles.

"Uh-huh. And I'm holding Jeremiah Bear. We're going for a walk along the river to have a picnic. See, this person is you waiting for us." A man stood in the distance with his arms open.

"I love it," he said softly, reaching for the picture. "I'll have to hang it on the fridge."

"Really?" She smiled wide. "I've never had a picture up on the fridge."

A funny look came over Daddy's face, but she didn't pay much attention. She was already starting another picture. This was fun.

"You miss Jeremiah Bear?"

"Uh-huh," she replied. "I used to hug him at night when I got scared."

"Do you still get scared at night?"

She frowned, not liking these questions. "Sometimes." She looked up at him as he sat down next to her once more.

"You know I'm here for you if you get scared, right, baby girl?"

"I know, Daddy." She smiled. "You're my very own Daddy bear."

He groaned but his eyes were warm as he leaned over and gave her a soft kiss on the forehead.

"I STINK."

As soon as the words left her mouth, she blushed bright red in embarrassment. What was wrong with her? Bear glanced away from his book to give her a look filled with surprise and amusement. She was still sitting on the sofa. She'd been drawing up a storm all afternoon. Bear had run out of room on the small fridge for her creations.

"I just...I mean..." She really wanted a bath. He'd given her a cloth to give herself a bit of a wipe, but it wasn't the same. "Maybe I could have a bath?"

And maybe he'd help her and she could entice him into another kiss like the one he'd given her yesterday. Oh hell, she was in so much trouble. She had no idea what she was doing.

"We don't exactly have a bath. Just an old tub I'd need to haul inside and heat up the water for."

"Oh, if it's too much trouble that's fine."

"I didn't say that. I don't want you getting in and out on your own, though. You could slip and fall."

"Perhaps you could help me then." She was trying for coy and sophisticated. She was pretty certain she did not pull it off.

But now that she'd said it, her body was filling with heat at the idea of him washing her. He looked at her thoughtfully. "I guess Daddy could give his little girl a bath."

She'd kind of been hoping Daddy would give his big girl a bath, but she'd take what she could get.

"All right. A short bath. That's all."

"Anything you say, Daddy."

He snorted. "If only I could believe that."

WHAT THE HELL was he thinking?

He heated up water to add to the bath and tried to ignore his hard dick pressing against his zipper. He had to be insane to agree to bathe her. He prided himself on his control and yet when it came to her...his control was wearing a little thin.

He was just a daddy giving his Little a bath.

Shit. How was he going to keep his need for her under control? Sure, he'd helped her wipe herself with a cloth, but he hadn't really looked.

He tested the water. He'd grabbed a washcloth, towel and soap already. "Okay, little girl, bath is ready." He turned to where she was sitting on the sofa. He reached for her, removing the blanket from over her lap. It was probably overkill since it was so hot in here, but he liked coddling her. She'd had precious little care in her life.

First, he removed her sweatshirt. Then her black t-shirt. He hated her in black. If she was his she'd wear bright, cheerful colors. She wasn't wearing a bra and as soon as her breasts were revealed, her pink nipples puckered.

She covered her breasts with her arm but he didn't linger. Instead, he helped her stand then crouched in front of her. "Hold onto my shoulders for balance."

She held onto him and stepped out of her panties, one foot at a time. He stood, but kept hold of her panties. Just as he'd suspected. "These are wet, baby girl."

"Oh God." She blushed bright red. "I'm so embarrassed."

He raised an eyebrow. "Why? Nothing sexier than knowing you want me." And knowing that was going to make it even harder to keep his hands off her.

"You think that's sexy?" she said hesitantly.

"Hell, yes."

He placed her panties on top of her other clothes then he helped her into the bath.

She sighed as the warm water lapped around her.

"Do you want your hair up?"

"Can I wash it? There's shampoo and conditioner in my toilet bag."

He thought about it, worried she might grow chilly with wet hair, but he could sit her down by the fire for a while and it would dry.

"Anything else you want from there?"

"Can you get my razor? I feel like Sasquatch. And I cannot believe I just said that to you."

He grinned. He liked that she didn't always have a filter on her mouth. She was real. There was no pretense. Not like there had been with Maria.

Put her out of your mind.

He should probably let her bathe herself, but he just couldn't manage it. He had to touch her. He looked through her luggage for the toilet bag. Grabbing it out, he drew out some shampoo, conditioner and a razor. He put them all by the bath then knelt beside it. He picked up the soap and washcloth, wetting them both then rubbing the soap against the washcloth until it got all sudsy.

"Lie back and rest your head on the lip of the bath, little one. Let Daddy wash you."

SHE LEANED BACK. He started washing along her chest then her arms, pulling one arm up then the other. She'd thought it might feel weird or embarrassing having him wash her. The tub was big enough that the water came up to her neck when she lay back, covering her completely.

"Sit forward, let me wash your back." She sat up. His gaze moved to her breasts, her stiff nipples. His gaze was caught on them as she leaned forward. He washed slowly down her back. Each stroke felt like he was stroking her pussy.

Oh man, she was so turned on. Too much more of this and she was going to take matters into her own hands.

"Lean back again."

She sat back and he moved to her legs, raising one and putting the foot on the edge of the bath. He washed her foot then worked his way down towards her pussy, stopping just short. Damn him.

She let out a little whimper of frustration.

"You all right, baby?" he asked. There was a hint of a grin on his face. "Your head okay?"

He moved to the other leg, raising it up, each brush of the washcloth getting closer and closer to her pussy.

"My head is just fine." She let out a groan as he placed her leg back into the water.

"You don't sound okay. Something has to be wrong." He surprised her by moving the washcloth to her breasts. He ran it over her nipple then around her breast and back over the nipple.

She bit her lip, unable to stop herself from arching her breasts up.

"Have you ever masturbated, Ellie?"

Oh my God.

"Bear! You can't ask me that."

"I just did. And you have ten seconds in which to answer me." His voice went all stern. Growly. Fuck, fuck, fuck. He'd moved the cloth to her other breast but now he was still.

"Or?" she asked.

"Or I'm going to tease you and leave you all hot and bothered without permission to come."

Permission to come? Shit. "You wouldn't!"

He just sent her a look.

"Of course, you would," she muttered. "You know that's sadistic, right? And how do you know I wouldn't just...just make myself come?"

"Because I would know and it would not go well for you."

She bit at her lip. "Yes, I've masturbated."

He started to move the washcloth over her nipple. Her pussy clenched, aching and empty. "What did you do when you masturbated?"

"Do we really have to talk about this?" she wailed. "It's private."

"It's nothing to be embarrassed about," he told her matter-of-factly.

"Oh, sure it's not, so do you masturbate?"

"Yep. Sure do."

Her jaw dropped open. Then interest filled her eyes. "Really? Can I watch?"

He let out a surprised bark of laughter. "What?"

"Oh. Sorry. God, I can't believe I just said that. Umm, I think I'm all clean now."

She tried to stand and he held her down with one hand on her tummy. "Stay where you are. Look at me."

She kept her gaze to the right, away from him.

"I have a lot of patience, Ellie. But even that will run out soon. And then you're going to be in trouble. Look at me."

She raised her gaze to his. "I'm so sorry I said that."

"Why?"

"Be-because we...I...it's not something I should have..."

"I brought up masturbation," he said simply. "Why should you be embarrassed over wanting to watch me?"

She could see he really meant that. And he was moving the washcloth down her stomach. Was he finally going to touch her there?

"What do you do when you masturbate?"

She groaned. "Bear, do I have to..."

"Tell me. You want to see me masturbate? I might consider allowing that but only after you do as I say."

"Oh hell," she muttered.

"Do you touch your breasts, Ellie? Do you caress them, cup them, run your fingers over your nipples?"

"I-I..." She licked her lips. "I sometimes pinch my nipples a little."

"Really? Like this?" He cupped her left breast with his free hand and lightly pinched her nipple.

She gasped, thrusting her hips up instinctively. "Oh my God. It feels different when you do it."

"Yeah?" He gave her other nipple a light pinch. "Different good or bad?"

"G-good. It feels a lot better when you do it."

"I'm glad." He moved the washcloth lower, down between her folds. She cried out as he ran it over her clit.

"Damn, you're responsive."

"Is that a good thing?" she asked, wanting to please him.

"It's a very good thing." He lay the cloth on the side of the bath. She nearly grabbed his hand and demanded he bring it back. But then she was glad she hadn't as he cupped her mound with his hand.

With his other hand he played with her nipple, rolling it between his finger and thumb. He ran one finger along her folds to her clit then flicked it lightly.

Oh hell. Oh hell.

"Anyone ever played with these nipples but you?" he asked.

Her breath was coming in sharp pants. "My boyfriend in high school squeezed my boob. It hurt and I was bruised for weeks."

"Asshole. These breasts need to be cherished. Worshipped. They should be licked and suckled often." He arranged her so she was half-sitting, her breasts partly exposed. Leaning down, he wrapped his lips around her right nipple and started sucking.

She let out a cry and arched up. "Bear!"

She was in heaven. Her body on fire. She never wanted him to stop. But it wasn't enough, she needed more. He strummed at her clit

"That...that...oh hell," she gasped as he lightly licked across her nipple.

"I'm a boob guy. I make no apologies for it. And your breasts are fucking magnificent."

"Not too small?"

"Nope. Perfect." He kissed his way across to the other nipple, lapping at it. "Every morning, I would wake up and suck on them, teasing them. Then once I had you all hot and bothered, I might press you back on the bed, push your legs up and tease your little clit with my tongue. Or I might finger fuck you until you were screaming. Or maybe I'd just roll you onto your back and fuck you."

"Oh God. You're killing me here."

"Good, because the feeling is mutual," he told her. "I've been in pain thinking about touching you, tasting you. I didn't want to scare you, though."

"You don't scare me, Bear. I feel so...so in need. Almost out of control. I haven't ever felt like this when I've touched myself."

"That's good."

"Can I touch you, though?" she asked on a gasp.

"Maybe later. Right now, this is about you."

She took in a sharp breath. She wasn't used to that.

"Don't think, baby. Just feel."

"I don't know how to not think," she told him. "I'm always thinking."

"But you don't have to think when I'm in charge, do you? When daddy is here, he does all the worrying."

"Does that...but we're not...I don't feel little right now."

"No, but that doesn't mean I'm not still in charge. Would you trust me to take control? To make the commands? Could you obey me in the bedroom as well?"

She thought that through. "You'll tell me what to do?"

"Yes. I'll take charge of it all."

"And you'll like that?"

He gave her a small grin. "Baby, I'm just waiting for you to say yes."

"Then yes. Please. I think it will make things easier on me if I don't have to worry about what to do with my hands or if I should kiss you or what I should be doing next."

"Then from now on, until such time as you decide otherwise, I'm in control in the bedroom as well, same safe word applies."

"Okay, Daddy."

"Good girl. Now, I just want you to relax. I'm going to do all the work. All you have to do is relax and let go. That's it."

Bear watched her as he moved his finger faster against her clit. He was on his knees now, bent over the tub. He leaned down and suckled on her nipple. He wasn't lying before. He adored breasts.

He could feel her breath coming in sharp, hard pants and he added more pressure to her clit.

"Bear! Bear!" she cried out as she came. God, he nearly came in his pants at the same time. He wanted to be inside her, wanted to feel her coming around his cock. But the last thing she needed right now was him taking her virginity.

But hell, playing with her sure was fun. He watched as a small smile curled up her lips. Yeah, he could do this all day long. He removed his fingers from her pussy, running them through the small curls there.

He tugged at them. "I'm going to use your razor to take this off later as well."

"Guys like that?"

He shrugged. He didn't want to talk about what other men might want. He didn't want to think about her with anyone else.

She was his.

No. That wasn't right. She couldn't be his. She wanted her freedom and she deserved it.

"I like it."

"Okay," she whispered, looking up so trustingly at him. "Thank you."

He grinned then leaned in to kiss her. "You're welcome."

He grabbed her razor and the soap. "Now put your legs up so I can shave them."

"Oh, you don't have to do that." She reached for the razor and he gave her a look. She dropped her hand into the water and lay back as he lifted her leg up to shave it.

"Little girls can't be trusted with sharp things," he told her. "Now, just lie back while I take care of you then we'll wash your hair and get you out of there. You'll be getting tired."

"I'm fine. I'm not tired."

Uh-huh. Of course, she wasn't. He quickly shaved her legs and then grabbed a cup to help wash her hair. Normally, he might take his time, savor the moment but he didn't want her getting cold. When her hair was washed, he wrapped a towel around it.

"I'm going to lift you out now, baby girl."

She held up her arms trustingly. Damn, she blew him away. He quickly lifted her out and dried her. Then he grabbed another towel and wrapped her up. He picked her up and carried her over to the fireplace. There was a rug on the floor in front of the fire and he sat her down.

"Stay here while I get your hair brush and the razor."

"Okay, Daddy."

He moved quickly, grabbing the stuff and the stool then brought them back, setting the stool behind her. He sat and pulled her back between his legs. Then he undid the towel around her hair and started to brush out the knots in her hair.

She sighed and he paused. "All right, baby?"

"Just happy, Daddy. Can't remember the last time someone did this for me."

It was on the tip of his tongue to tell her he'd do it for her every time if she'd just stay with him.

Can't happen.

She turned to look at him questioningly. "Daddy?"

He realized he'd stilled. "Sorry, baby girl. I was thinking." He brushed her hair until it was tangle free then got up and grabbed a blanket off the bed.

"I want you to lie down on your back," he told her in a low voice as he pulled the towel off her. She gasped a little, looking embarrassed as she sat naked in front of him. Her hands creeped up to her breasts.

"I've just washed every inch of you. There's no need to be embarrassed. Now lay back and I'll put this blanket on you."

He watched hungrily as she lay down. Her hair spilled around her and he gathered it up so it wasn't lying next to her skin, fanning it out on the rug beneath her so it would dry more quickly.

"Warm enough?" he murmured.

"Yes," she replied, her cheeks slightly flushed. With embarrassment or arousal he wasn't sure.

"Good. Bring your legs together and bend them, feet on the floor, then let your knees drop open like you would at the gynecologist."

"I've never been to one."

"What?" He stared at her in shock.

"Well, I've never had sex before so didn't see much need."

He shook his head. "You still need to be checked over. Your parents ought to be shot for not taking care of you properly."

"Can we talk about something other than my parents right now?"

He nodded. "Sure, baby. Do as I've said now."

She looked uncertain but raised her legs up then dropped them to the sides. A shiver rocked her.

"Too cold?" He looked up at her in concern.

"No. I just...this is a little embarrassing."

"Like I said, nothing is embarrassing between a daddy and his little one." He rubbed his hand over the top of her thigh soothingly. Then he grabbed the can of shaving cream he'd found in her toilet bag. She obviously used it for her legs, but it would work well for this.

He lathered her up and started to shave her pussy.

"Just stay very still and Daddy will get all this hair off this pretty, plump pussy." Her legs trembled and he heard her breath coming faster. As he finished, he drew the lips of her pussy apart to get any stray hairs, but mostly so he could check how wet she was. Her lips glistened, her clit was swollen, peeking out of its hood.

"Uh-oh, somebody likes having Daddy shave their pussy. Look how wet you are."

"Oh God," she groaned.

He lay on his stomach between her legs and spread her wide, inspecting her. "Ask Daddy to make you come."

"W-what?"

"Ask me to make you come. Ask me very nicely and I might just lick you into orgasm."

There was a beat of silence. "Please, Daddy, will you make me come?" she asked in a hesitant voice.

"Hmm. Not quite. Say, please Daddy, will you lick my little pussy and make me come all over your tongue."

"I can't say that!"

He had to hide a grin at her shocked voice. Then he schooled his face into a stern look and sat up so he was gazing down at her. "Do you want to come, Ellie?"

She whimpered and nodded.

"Then you know what to do, don't you? You need to learn to obey Daddy."

She flung an arm over her eyes. "Please Daddy, will you lick my little p-pussy and make me come all over your t-tongue?"

"It would be my pleasure."

He laid back between her legs, parting her plump lips. He leaned in, taking a long, leisurely lick of her juices. He cupped her breasts, playing with her nipples as he explored her pussy.

He sighed in satisfaction as the taste of her burst along his tongue. Her small whimpers filled the room, and his cock throbbed with need. Damn, he was going to have to dive naked into the snow at this point to cool himself off.

Circling her clit, he listened to her cries deepen, her breathing grow more erratic. She shifted around on the rug, but otherwise she was quiet.

So this is what he had to do to get her to be quiet? He smiled.

Truthfully, the amount she talked didn't worry him. He'd thought it would have. He was a pretty quiet guy, generally. But it was nice to have someone fill the silence.

He flicked his tongue over her clit and she let out a loud cry, her hips thrusting up. He moved his tongue around, circling her clit then running the flat of it over the top before flicking it firmly.

"Oh God. Oh God, Bear. That feels fucking amazing. Please. Please. I can't...please, I can't."

He knew she was close. Punishing her by withholding orgasm was going to be hard when she reached her peak so quickly. She was so honest. There was no pretense to her.

He moved his finger to circle her entrance then pushed it slightly inside her, thrusting it back and forth gently as he drove his tongue against her clit. Faster. Harder. Until she screamed with her release. He could feel her pulsate around the tip of his finger and couldn't help but imagine what she would feel like around his cock.

He continued to lick her until her breathing calmed then he knelt and stripped off his shirt, needing to cool off a bit, before he lay beside her on his back.

"Oh my," she said in a breathless voice.

"Oh my," he repeated with amusement. Sometimes the things she came out with were hilarious.

"So how does that rate in comparison to what you've had before?" he asked her with a small grin on his face.

"Rate?" she asked. "It doesn't even rate on the same scale. What I gave myself was barely a one, what you just gave me was an eighty-five, at least."

"Eighty-five?" he mused. "I'm going to have to up my game, then aren't I?" He lightly pinched her nipple. "I've got to at least get two hundred, right?"

She rolled her eyes. "The scale was a one to ten scale, you know."

"I know. But a man's gotta have goals."

"That was...beyond anything I'd ever imagined."

He rolled onto his side and gave her a long, lingering kiss before pulling back reluctantly.

She ran her hand over his shoulder and down his chest. "My God, you're beautiful."

He gave a surprised laugh. "It's not me who is the beautiful one, sweetheart."

She smiled. "I guess men don't like being called beautiful. But you are. You're hot and rugged and sweet and sexy and kind. Why don't you have a girlfriend?"

He stiffened slightly at her words. Because he couldn't trust anyone's motives. But he trusted her. Jesus, he'd known her just a few days. But they'd been together almost every minute of those days. Hell, they'd probably spent more time together than a couple who had been dating for a month.

She leaned in and latched onto his nipple and he groaned, his attention diverted from his thoughts. Especially as she licked at his nipple, her other hand running down his abs, towards his...

BEAR ROLLED her gently onto her back. She opened her mouth to protest but he followed her down, lying over her, his weight resting on his forearms which lay on either side of her head, his legs between hers, his cock pressing against her pussy. And there was no mistaking that there was something very hard and very large pressed against her.

"So, you carry bananas in your pocket?" she joked, feeling slightly breathless.

"Baby, if you can't tell the difference between a banana and a cock, we have some problems."

"You might have to educate me."

"First of all, there is nothing squishy about my cock."

"Got it," she replied as he pushed against her.

"You cannot peel my cock."

"Uh-huh."

"You squeeze it and you're likely to get a whole different reaction from doing that with a banana."

"How is this conversation turning me on?" she muttered.

He grinned down at her. "Biting down is a hard limit. You bite down on my cock, and I'm going to tie you up, put a clit tickler on you and keep you on the edge of orgasm all day."

"Got it, no eating the banana, umm I mean cock."

"Of course, you are welcome to suck, lick, and run your hand up and down it."

"I cannot wait. What about the accompanying mangoes?" she asked.

"Mangoes? We have got to work on your dirty talk."

"Ooh, is that what this is? I've never engaged in dirty talk before." She grinned.

He quirked one eyebrow. "I couldn't tell."

She slapped his shoulder playfully.

"Just for reference, if they were mangoes, I would have some serious issues with walking normally."

"Grapes then?" she asked with mock-innocence.

"Grapes!" He gave her an outraged look. "Woman, you are this close to ending up over my knee." He held up his thumb and forefinger so they were an inch apart.

"I certainly hope that's not an indication of your banana size."

"You know damn well it's not," he muttered.

"I really think I should help you with that fruit salad problem you have going on."

He groaned at her words. "Sweetheart, right now I want nothing more than to spend the afternoon with you in bed."

"There's a but coming, isn't there?"

"I don't think now is the time for me to be taking your virginity."

It smarted a little. She knew he was just trying to protect her. But she guessed she wanted him to be so overcome with lust he couldn't think of anything but taking her. Then again, the attention he'd given her was like nothing she'd experienced before.

He put her needs first. And she'd never had someone like that in her life, had she?

"But we don't need to fuck for me to help you with your little problem."

"Can you please not call it a *little* problem? You'll give me a complex."

She giggled. She was aware that he wasn't saying no. "Please, Bear. I want to do this."

He rolled away from her and disappointment flooded her. He lay with his arm over his face. "You are fucking killing me here."

He hadn't left, though. She rolled to her side and slowly reached a hand under his jeans. "Please let me."

He dropped his arm to peer out at her. "Like I can fucking say no to you?"

She grinned. "Really? I'll keep that in mind."

He pointed a finger at her. "To a point. I won't let you risk yourself."

"I hardly think giving you a blow job is much of a risk." She undid his jeans and he helped her by raising his hips so she could lower them. He was going commando. Her breath sucked in at the sight of him. Nope, nothing little about his problem.

"Hand job," he countered.

"What?" she asked, distracted. She wrapped her hand around his cock. It twitched and she nearly giggled. Okay, she had to get her shit together. She might be inexperienced, but she was pretty certain giggling at a guy's dick was a big no-no. It wasn't that she found it funny. She was just nervous as hell. She'd never sucked a man's cock. She'd never even touched one before. Yep, this was a whole new ballgame. He was warmer than she'd thought. Smooth. Firm. There was no hair around his genitals, did he remove it?

"You're going to give me a hand-job."

"All right. I, umm, don't really know what I'm doing, though."

"Fuck, baby. Not much you can do wrong," he groaned as she lightly squeezed him. "Run your hand up and down my shaft. Yeah, that's it. It's not going to take much for me to come. This is going to be the world's shortest fucking hand job."

She smiled at that. Although she didn't want it to end too quickly. She wanted to keep touching him, giving him pleasure. He had an unguarded look on his face, he was relaxed. She liked it. She continued to run her hand up and down his dick.

"What else should I be doing?"

He looked at her. "It's a turn-on, knowing this is your first hand-job, you know, that right?"

"Really?" she asked. "I thought it would be turn-off for most guys, me not knowing what I'm doing."

She'd been starting to think she might have to look into lessons or something. Or some sort of instructional video online.

"Nope, fucking turn-on knowing I'm your first."

"I want you to be my first in everything," she whispered.

His face tightened and she wasn't sure what that look on his face was. Did he not like that idea? Was it something he didn't want?

She hated being so insecure.

"Lean in and lick my nipple," he commanded instead of responding to what she'd just revealed. "Play with me like I did with you."

Okay, that she could do. She leaned in and ran her tongue over his nipple. He groaned. "I didn't know that nipples were as sensitive for men as they are for women."

"Don't know about other men, that's not really something we sit around and discuss, but I like my nipples being played with."

Then that's what she'd do. Because she wanted to please him. She wanted to make him feel as good as he had her.

So, she suckled on his nipple then lapped at it with her tongue.

"Don't stop using your hand on me," he groaned.

She realized then that her hand had stilled. Shit. She was already failing hand job 101. "Sorry," she said hastily.

"Nothing to be sorry about," he told her. "I get it. My nipple is pretty mesmerizing."

She snorted. "Yep, it pulled me into its orbit and I couldn't break free. It's like a sick obsession."

"I have heard that more than I can say."

Okay, she didn't like that. She narrowed her gaze at him. "That so?"

"It was a joke," he said hastily.

"Good, because I might be a virgin but even I know it's bad form to talk about your other lovers when your current lover has her hand around your cock."

"Very bad form."

She smiled then leaned up to kiss him. He met her halfway, his tongue sweeping inside to play with hers and she realized she was so taken with the kiss that she'd stopped her movements along his cock again.

"You're distracting me," she complained after pulling away from him.

"Don't want that," he panted. His breath was coming faster. His skin glistening with sweat. "I'm close, sweetheart."

"Please, could I taste you?"

"You really want to taste me?" He looked surprised.

"Women don't want that?"

"Not the ones I've been with." He grimaced as he realized what he said. "Sorry."

"I want to. Please. Please let me."

He groaned. "Fuck. Never had anyone beg to taste me. Christ, what are you doing to me? All right. But take it nice and slow. Take me into your mouth and keep using your hand."

She scooted down eagerly, taking the first few inches of his dick into her mouth.

"Now suck on me, baby. That's it. Yeah, run your hand up and down my dick. Oh, fuck yeah. You have no idea how good that feels. Get ready, I'm about to come. You can still pull back if you need to."

He thrust up slightly, and found his release. She swallowed him down, loving the noises he made, knowing she'd brought him as much pleasure as he had her. She kept hold of him even after he'd completely spent. Then she pulled back, licking the head.

"Baby, oh shit, you have to stop that."

"You haven't gone down," she pointed out, staring at his still-hard cock.

"Yeah, well, I don't think once with you is enough for the old fella."

"Old fella?" She giggled. "You're not that old."

"I am in comparison to you," he grumbled. "Get up here and stop staring at him. He's going to get a complex."

"Jeez, I can't call him small, can't stare at him. He's got issues."

He snorted. "Move up here, I want to cuddle you."

He drew her up so she lay sprawled over his chest. He wrapped his arm around her and placed his hand on her neck, massaging lightly.

"All right? Not hurting anywhere?"

"Bear, I'm not fragile."

"Never said you were. But you were just injured."

"I don't need you to baby me." She realized what she'd just said and blushed. "Well, you know what I mean."

"I haven't been babying you, although I certainly can. I'm sure

I can fashion a diaper and find something that might work as a pacifier."

She leaned up to glare down at him. He grinned at her.

"Stop joking around. I don't go that young when I'm little."

"Come here." He positioned her against his chest once more and placed a kiss on the top of her head. "You know I only want to give you what you need."

Made for a nice change from having her needs completely ignored. Even if it was a bit of an adjustment for her.

"So...how was that on a scale?" she asked.

"Oh, definitely a nineteen."

"What?"

"Out of twenty," he added with a chuckle.

"Hmm, seems I'm going to need practice. I wonder where I can find a willing partner."

He smacked his hand down sharply on her bottom. "What was that?"

"I didn't mean it, sir! You're the only partner I need. I only want to practice my skills with your banana and mangoes."

She giggled as he groaned.

6

―――――

"**W**ill you sleep with me tonight?" Ellie asked him as she lay in bed that night. It was probably silly to feel so shy when he'd had his mouth on her pussy earlier. But what if he said no? She was going to feel embarrassed and rejected.

He rubbed his chin, looking tired. He couldn't be getting much rest in that chair. Guilt filled her. She wanted to take care of him. Wanted to do something for him.

Well, you could always give him another hand job.

Jeez, was she turning into a hussy or what?

"Not sure that's a good idea."

Her heart plummeted. He was rejecting her. What they'd done earlier meant nothing to him. He was probably grateful things hadn't gone any further than they had.

"My control only goes so far and it would be too tempting, lying next to you."

She sucked in a breath. "You still want me?"

His gaze narrowed. "Still want you? I want you even more than I did before and I didn't think that was possible." He shifted around on the armchair. "Think I might need another cold walk outside just so I can get more comfortable."

"What does walking outside have to do with getting comfortable?"

He raised one eyebrow. "Ever heard of someone needing a cold shower because they were aroused?"

"What? Oh, yes. Do you mean every time you've gone outside it's because..." she trailed off.

"Well, not every time," he said dryly. "But yeah."

"Oh."

"You really thought I didn't want you? The taste of you on my tongue is going to haunt me. If I close my eyes, I can hear the little cries you make, see the way you tense up just before you come, feel you pulsating around my finger. And damn do I wish that had been my dick inside you."

"Oh," she said again. *Say something sensible, Ellie.* "That sounds nice. Could we do that?"

He laughed. "Baby, I'm trying to be good here."

"Being good is overrated," she told him.

"Oh, is it? Because being naughty just gets you spanked."

Yeah, well, those few swats he'd given her earlier had just stirred her arousal so that didn't sound like much of a threat.

"You're not up to sex yet, Ellie. It's your first time. It should be special."

"But I'm not sure I can sleep like this. I think you should climb into bed with me and see what you can do to soothe me."

He shook his head but he was grinning. "You are such trouble. I am not having sex with you."

She sighed. "Fine. But that doesn't mean we couldn't do what we did earlier, right? I mean, I think I need some more practice."

"Not tonight. You're tired and you need to rest."

She gave him her best pleading look.

"But I will sleep with you. Only sleep. And if you try for

anything more, you're going to feel my hand on your backside again."

Promises. Promises.

She didn't say that out loud, though. She wasn't that silly.

"You're not always going to get your way, little girl."

"Of course not, Daddy," she said with mock-innocence.

"Brat," he said affectionately. But he stripped off his clothes. This time he was wearing boxers, which he left on as he climbed into bed beside her. She snuggled in against him and he wrapped a wide arm around her. A sense of rightness stole over her.

"You're so warm."

"And you're freezing. Why didn't you tell me you were so cold?"

"I didn't feel cold until you got in. You're like a furnace." She rested her head on his chest with a happy sigh. "I love it when you hold me. I've never been held like this."

He kissed the top of her head. "I like it too, baby girl. Now go to sleep."

She yawned. "Not tired. Tell me a story."

"You just yawned. Sleep."

"No."

"Do you need me to warm your bottom for you?" His voice was a low rumble. Hmm, maybe that would be nice. But then again, he didn't sound to happy with her.

"No." She was silent for a moment. "But I really want a story first. Please, Daddy? Then I'll go straight to sleep."

His sigh was long and exaggerated. "Fine. Once upon a time there was a very patient Daddy—"

"Did he have a beard?"

"Yes."

"Ooh, and was he sexy?"

He pulled her into him and laid two sharp smacks onto her ass.

"Hey! No fair. You didn't say I couldn't ask questions, Daddy."

"Don't interrupt me again, or you'll be going to sleep with a red bottom and no story," he warned.

"I thought you weren't going to spank me while I was healing."

"I thought you were feeling all better?" he questioned her. "You can't have it both ways, little girl. And before you say anything, remember what happens when you lie."

She sighed. "I do feel a lot better."

"What about your headaches? Tiredness? Dizzy spells?"

She didn't really want to answer. But she knew she had to. "I'm still getting headaches."

"And what helps those headaches?"

"The medicine."

"And?"

"And a nap," she answered sulkily.

"Which is why you still need plenty of rest," he told her. "And don't think I've forgotten that dizzy spell when you got up from lying on the rug earlier."

"That was just from moving too fast."

"Uh-huh," he said dryly. "Now, am I telling the rest of this story without interruption or are you getting a spanking?"

"Story," she said quickly.

"Right, now, where was I?"

"There was a beautiful princess who never got spanked because she was the best girl in the world."

He chuckled. "She is beautiful and a good girl, but she will most definitely be getting spanked."

"Just in the story, though right, Daddy?"

"Oh, didn't I tell you? This is based on a true story. Because the naughty little princess went riding her horse without telling anyone or taking her phone and got lost and the very patient daddy had to rescue her. When he learned how foolish she had been with her safety, he put her over his knees and raised her skirt to bare her bottom then he laid several hard smacks to her ass.

The princess protested that she shouldn't be subjected to such a punishment, after all she was a princess. But the daddy didn't care about that. All he cared about was keeping the princess safe. And he knew the best way to ensure that she never got into trouble again was to give her a good hard spanking. So, he smacked her bottom until it was bright red and she was sobbing and remorseful. And when it was over, he held her in his arms and rocked her and told her that she was too important to be so reckless. The end."

"No, that's not the end."

"No?"

"No, it always goes 'and they lived happily ever after'." She yawned again and snuggled in against him as she fell off asleep.

BEAR LAY THERE, with her tucked in against him unable to sleep.

Happily ever after.

If only it was that simple.

⁓

"I WANT TO COME."

"No."

She crossed her arms over her chest. "What if you need my help?"

He shot her a look. Yeah, okay, she wasn't likely to need her help. But still, she didn't want to be left in the cabin on her own while he went to check the state of the road.

They'd been in this cabin for five days now. And truth be told, it wasn't that she was concerned about being on her own, she just wanted to be with him.

She was also worried that the road would be clear and this would be the end of their time together.

"What if I need you?"

"I'm only going to be gone about two hours, Ellie," he said patiently. "You'll be okay. I'll be back before you know it. Now, do you need anything before I go?"

She was up and dressed, sitting on the sofa again. She was feeling loads better, although she was still getting headaches. She hadn't had one today, though. So maybe they were disappearing.

"No."

"All right. I want you to stay inside the cabin and rest. Understand me?"

"Yes, Daddy."

He came over and kissed her gently. "Be a good girl and Daddy will be back soon."

"All right, drive carefully," she said anxiously.

"I will be fine." He moved to the door and left without another word. She looked around the cabin. What was she going to do for a few hours?

BEAR PULLED up outside the cabin. The road was still a bit of a mess. There was no getting through until the tree was cleared away. He could try going the other way and heading to the city, but that was a long drive for Ellie and they were okay here for a bit longer. He'd called Sanctuary to let them know what was going on.

And if truth be told, he wasn't really ready for his time here to be over. She'd buried herself deep under his skin and he didn't want to let go. Even though he knew he had to. She'd made it clear she wasn't looking for anything permanent.

He opened his truck door, eager to see her. As soon as he climbed out, though, he knew she'd disobeyed him. He spotted some pieces of bread over towards the woods and some small footprints dotting the snow between the cabin and the bread.

He shook his head. Little brat. Had she really thought he wouldn't find out?

He walked up the porch steps. He'd obviously done her a disservice by waiting to dispense discipline. If she was well enough to move around outside, she was well enough for a proper spanking.

ELLIE WAS SITTING in the armchair, trying to read when Bear opened the door. She was having trouble concentrating on the words and as soon as he walked in, she instantly forgot what she was reading.

"Daddy!" she squealed. Then she jumped up and rushed towards him.

"No running," he barked at her as she flung herself against him. "Damn it, Ellie. You're going to hurt yourself."

"Pfft, I'm fine. You worry too much. How was the drive? Was the road still a mess?"

"Yep, tree is still down. We can probably make it back the other way towards the city, but it would take us a long time. Best to wait until the road is cleared, I think, and head towards Wishingbone."

"I'm in no rush to go anywhere."

He tilted her head back gently and leaned down to kiss her. "You're not eager to start your new life as a single, independent woman?"

It was what she should want. What she did want. Didn't she?

Somehow, she wasn't so sure anymore. Because when she thought about her life without him in it, it felt dark and lonely.

But he thankfully didn't wait for her reply, instead swinging her up into his arms and carrying her towards the bed.

"So, you want to tell me what you got up to while I was away?" he asked.

Uh-oh. There was a note to his voice that told her she should proceed with caution.

"I, umm, might have done a little cleaning."

"A little cleaning, huh? I think my idea of a little and yours might differ greatly. This place is practically sparkling." He sat on the bed, but didn't keep her on his lap. Instead he stood her between his outstretched legs and reached for the top of her sweatpants, pulling them down.

"Any headaches?" he asked calmly. What was going on?

"No, none. I feel great. I promise."

"Great, huh? That's good."

What was he doing? Why was he taking off her pants? Her body stirred. Was he finally going to fuck her? Yeah, right. It was more likely he was stripping her off for a nap. He leaned down and she held onto his shoulders as he pulled the pants off each foot.

"I got a little bored. Are you mad?" she asked, trying to gauge his mood.

"Mad, no. I'm not mad. What else did you get up to?"

Okay, she really didn't want to answer that question. "I don't want a nap."

"Well, what you want isn't always what you need. And you might feel differently after."

After? After what?

"You haven't answered me. What else did you do?"

Oh crap. She looked down into his stern eyes and she just knew he knew. "How did you know?"

"How doesn't matter. Tell me," his voice was a low growl.

"There were these squirrels. I thought they might be hungry. I dressed up real warm, I promise. And I only went as far as the end of the clearing. You wouldn't want me to let them go hungry, would you?"

"Leaving some bread out for them couldn't have waited until I got home?" His voice was patient. Calm.

And somehow, she thought it was the calm before the storm.

She bit her lip. "I guess that was an option. I was just so excited when I saw them out there and I didn't really want to wait."

"And you didn't think about the fact that you had been told to stay inside? That you don't have any warm clothes? That you could have slipped and fallen and been stuck out there for hours?"

"You shouldn't always think the worst, Daddy."

"Oh, I can see that I need to, since you obviously don't." He gave her a stern look. "This was a very serious breach of rules, little girl. So far, you've just been given a few swats because I've been waiting until you recovered. Obviously, that was a mistake. If you're well enough to clean and be naughty, you're well enough for a spanking. So, you're getting twenty-five with my hand. Fifteen for going outside when you were told to stay inside, ten for the other rules you broke."

"Daddy, no, that's way too many."

"Believe me, baby, this is me going easy on you. If I wasn't worried about pushing you too hard, you'd be getting much more. Daddy would be getting his belt."

BEAR GLARED at her as she gave him her best puppy dog eyes. He wasn't giving in this time.

"I'm not used to sitting around. I'm used to doing things. I'm used to being useful. And I feel good now. So, when I got up to use the toilet and I saw that there was a sink full of dishes I just figured I'd help you."

He hated that she kept thinking she owed him something.

"It doesn't feel right to just sit here while you do everything," she told him.

He got it. She had basically lived a life of servitude. She

certainly wasn't used to anyone doing anything for her. It didn't mean he had to like it. And it didn't mean that it was going to continue.

How could he get her to see that taking care of her made him happy? That he wasn't keeping some sort of damn ledger that said who owed who what?

He cared about Ellie. More than he thought he would care about a woman again. But it wouldn't be fair of him to talk her into something more. She had just gotten out of a controlling relationship. She had escaped because she wanted a chance to be on her own. To know what it was like to be independent.

She was the woman for him. He knew that. But he also knew that he had to give her a chance to live life the way that she wanted to. Otherwise she would always wonder and one day she might come to resent him.

This is why it was better to never love than to love and lose.

He sucked in a breath. Fuck. He loved her. Fate sure did love to fuck him over. He'd fallen in love with a woman that he was going to have to let go.

"Daddy, you okay?" she asked worriedly, patting his shoulder soothingly.

Shit. He needed to get his head back in the game.

"Yeah. Sorry. Just thinking about all the ways you might have hurt yourself today."

She bit her lip worriedly.

"Ellie, you might feel better, but I don't want you pushing things too far and having your health go backwards. That's completely unacceptable to me."

He pointed a finger at her. "You agreed that I would be in charge. While we are here, I make the rules. And I enforce them." He patted his lap. "Come lay yourself over my lap, little girl."

· · ·

SHE HAD to hold back a whimper as she climbed onto his lap. Somehow, she'd managed to fool herself into thinking he'd just give her a couple of swats or a scolding for breaking the rules today. She realized she'd been lulled into a false sense of security.

Bear arranged her so her head and torso rested on the bed on one side of him, and her legs on the other side. He even handed her a pillow.

"Put this under your head," he ordered.

"Daddy?" she asked.

"Yes," he replied as he pushed her panties down her legs. Oh God.

"Will you hold me after?" she asked in a small voice.

He paused then he rubbed her bottom. "Baby, I will always hold you after."

"You're really not mad?"

"I'm not mad at you. I'm upset because you disobeyed me and you could have hurt yourself. But I was never angry. You need to know that I will always follow through when you break a rule. Understand?"

"All right."

"You think you can keep your hands out in front of you or you want me to hold them?"

Have him hold them? She wasn't sure, but she didn't really like the idea of that. At least until she knew what she was dealing with. "I can do it, Daddy."

"Okay, I won't make you count this time since it's your first real punishment. You remember to use your safe word if anything other than your bottom starts to hurt."

"Yes." The knowledge that she had a safeword squashed some of the nerves dancing inside her.

"Good. Let's get this done with so I can give you those cuddles."

He smacked his hand down heavily. One smack. Two. She

cried out. It smarted. He seemed to be smacking harder than yesterday. After five, she was squirming.

"Daddy, no! It's enough."

"No, it's not. You have twenty more, baby. How is your head?"

She wished she could lie, but she knew that would get her in worse trouble. "It's okay."

He was rubbing her bottom as he spoke and that was kind of nice. In fact, it was starting to make her clit tingle. Hmm, perhaps if he kept doing that then this spanking wouldn't be so bad. But then his hand landed on her bottom again. Five sharp smacks that had her kicking her feet and little cries escaping unbidden from her lips. The sting was starting to really burn. Unable to stop herself, she reached back to cover her poor bottom with her hands.

"Uh-uh, keep those hands away." He caught them in the small of her back, holding them pinned against her as his hand continued to lay spank after spank on her vulnerable ass.

She tried desperately to rock her way off his lap. Unfortunately, she didn't manage to get far, he pressed her hands down against her back, holding her steady as he continued to lay into her ass. And yet despite the pain, or maybe because of it, her nipples were hard, her clit throbbing.

It was the damnedest thing. She wanted him to stop. She wanted to get away from that punishing hand...and yet, at the same time her body thrummed with arousal.

Tears dripped down her face, soaking the pillow beneath her. Finally, she just gave in and lay there, unable to do anything but cry. Several more spanks landed then he stopped and rubbed her lower back soothingly. Her poor bottom throbbed with a pain that seemed to sink in deep. And this was just one part of her punishment?

Crap.

"That's it, baby. Good girl. You were such a good girl to take your spanking so well," he crooned to her as she continued to cry.

Then he rolled her over and gently sat her up. She hissed as her bottom came into contact with his lap and he chuckled.

"Not funny, Daddy. I won't be able to sit for a week!"

"Oh, I very much doubt it will be that long," he told her. "That was a pretty easy punishment."

Easy? Was he kidding her? But before she could complain about that assessment, he moved, lying on his back with her lying on top of him. He rubbed her back soothingly as she sniffled against his chest.

"You took that very well, baby girl. I'm proud of you."

"It hurt." She heard the childish note in her voice.

"It was meant to."

"It wasn't like I thought. Those other spanks, they...umm...well..."

"They aroused you?" he guessed.

She squirmed on top of him. "Does that make me weird?"

"Not at all, baby. Lots of people find pleasure in pain. Are you wet right now? Did that spanking turn my little girl on?"

"Bear! You can't ask me that!" God, even if she hadn't already been turned on, she would be now.

"If you're not going to answer me then Daddy has no choice but to do an inspection." He gently rolled her onto her back. She was dressed in just her t-shirt and sweater, her panties down round her knees. He sat and stripped her panties off, ignoring the way she winced and hissed as her hot bottom touched the mattress beneath her.

"Put your legs together then bend them and drop them to the sides, just like I taught you," he ordered.

She gave a little whimper but did what he said. God, this was embarrassing. It was also a complete turn-on. There was something about being ordered to expose herself that just did it for her.

He knelt on the bed between her legs and looked down at her. "I think you got very turned on by your naughty girl spanking. Look at all this moisture." He parted her lips with and ran his finger down her folds then held it up, glistening with her dew.

She watched as he sucked on his fingers. "Yum. I wonder if you're going to get turned on every time I spank you. Or if you'll react this way with a harder punishment. Like when I use my belt."

"I'm not sure I want to find out," she muttered.

"Well, don't disobey Daddy again over a health and safety rule and you won't." He gave her a stern look.

"I'm sorry, Daddy."

"Like I said, you were already forgiven before the spanking. Although don't forget you've got another spanking coming." He eyed her. "Unless your head is sore? How are you feeling? Do you need any pain relief?"

"Yes."

"For your head?" He looked slightly alarmed.

"No, for my bottom."

"I don't administer pain relief for naughty bottoms," he informed her. He was rubbing his thumb around her clit as he spoke. "You feel all right everywhere else?"

Her breath was quickening and she arched her hips up. "Daddy?"

"Yes."

"There's somewhere else I ache."

"Really? Where is that?" He gave her an innocent look she didn't buy for a minute; he knew exactly what he was doing to her.

"Right where you're touching."

"Oh." He looked down at her pussy. "Yes, your little clit is all swollen, isn't it? I bet it would like to feel my tongue playing with it."

"Oh, yes, please."

"Hmm, too bad you've been naughty. I don't give orgasms after a punishment."

She cried out as he moved his hand away, thumping her fists against the bed. "That's so unfair."

"And throwing a tantrum is definitely not going to get you what you want," he told her sternly. "Now, I think you could use some time in the corner." He pointed at an empty corner in the room. He couldn't be serious!

"Get yourself into the corner. Hold your t-shirt and sweater up over your bottom. I want your nose in the corner, your legs spread wide, and that ass sticking out. Go. Now."

Well, crap seemed like he really was serious.

∾

"Come here, baby girl."

Oh, thank God that was over. Corner time sucked.

Especially when she was made to hold her t-shirt and sweater up high so her bare, throbbing bottom was on display as she rested her forehead against the corner of the room and pushed her butt out.

It was humiliating.

She dropped her clothing as she turned.

"Who said you could let go of the t-shirt?" he asked in a deep voice.

Well, crap. She grabbed it, pulling it up so her pussy and ass were exposed once more. Yep, corner time sucked.

He crooked a finger at her, then pointed to the space in front of him where he sat on the armchair. She came and stood between his open legs. He reached around and grabbed her ass cheeks firmly. She sucked in a breath. It was painful, but it also sent waves of heat rushing through her body.

"What did you think of corner time?" he asked her.

"I hated it."

"Did you? Your pussy says otherwise. I could see how wet your lips were from here."

"Oh God, the things you say to me," she groaned.

"How are you doing? Any pain?" He watched her carefully.

She just gave him a look. He smiled. "I meant, other than your bottom. That was only ten swats. Can't hurt that much."

"Maybe I should smack your bottom and see if you think it hurts." Fact was, it didn't hurt that much. It was the corner time combined with the unrelieved arousal rocking her body that had her pouting.

"Other than my bottom, I'm not in any pain."

She loved how he took care of her, even when he was punishing her. "Good. Now thank Daddy for your punishment." He removed one hand from her ass and pushed it up under her t-shirt to lightly pinch her nipple.

She groaned. He squeezed one ass cheek. Hard. She hissed, moving up onto her tiptoes in an effort to get away. It didn't work, of course.

"Little miss, thank Daddy for your spanking."

"Thank you, Daddy, for spanking me."

"Good girl." He eased off on the tight hold. "Take your sweater and t-shirt off."

She eagerly pulled them off and threw it away.

"Is my girl cold?" he asked, staring at her stiff nipples.

"They're not hard because they're cold, Daddy." Was he actually going to let her come? *Please. Please.*

"Offer your breast to me."

Offer it to him? She was puzzled for a minute then hesitantly reached up and cupped it, holding it up.

"That's it, now guide it to my mouth." He was so tall that he actually had to lean down to take her nipple into his mouth. He immediately started to suckle. Arousal flooded her, making her knees weak.

He seemed to sense this, though and wrapped his hands around her waist to hold her up.

"Easy, baby," he murmured as he moved to her other breast. She immediately cupped it, holding it up for him. "Fuck, you have perfect breasts. I'm starting to hate this no orgasm after a punishment rule."

"We could ignore it just this once, Daddy."

He pulled back with a groan. "Nope. Not happening. But damn, you tempt me. Let's get some clothes on you before I completely lose my mind."

Seemed only fair since she'd already lost hers.

7

She awoke with a flush of pleasure. She gasped as something ran over her swollen clit. Opening her eyes, she looked around, realizing it was early morning. But Bear wasn't lying beside her as he had been when they'd gone to sleep.

Obviously, he'd woken up with something other than sleep on his mind. She gasped as he lapped at her clit, his finger slid partially into her pussy, hitting her barrier and withdrawing. He played with her clit. Tapping it with his tongue, then pulling back when she got close to completion. Totally ignoring her groan of protest, he lightly circled it while his fingers pushed partially in and out of her passage.

Her pleasure grew, her entire body shaking with tremble after tremble, until finally she reached that peak. The crash was breathtaking. She let out a scream as she fell over the edge into bliss. He continued to lick at her until she collapsed, her body goo.

Bear moved up the bed and lay on his side next to her. He leaned in and gave her a light kiss. She could taste herself on his lips. "Good morning, baby."

God, how could he wake up looking this good? She knew she had to look a mess.

"Good morning, Daddy," she said happily moving into his embrace. She loved waking up next to him. Although this might be her very favorite way to wake up. "That was a nice way to wake up."

"Nice? Just nice?" He tickled her, pretending to be insulted. She erupted into laughter.

"Sorry. Sorry. It wasn't nice. It was tremendous. Fantastic. Amazing. The best I've ever had."

He stopped tickling her so he could kiss her. "It was the only you've ever had."

And the only she ever wanted to have. Except she couldn't say that to him. Because she couldn't ask him for more than this. He'd told her he wasn't looking for a relationship. And neither was she. Except now it didn't seem so important to stand on her own two feet. To be alone. To look after just herself. She wanted to take care of him. Be with him. Love him.

Oh hell, did she love him?

"Baby, you okay?" he asked, tilting her face up and look at her in concern.

"I'm fine." She smiled at him. "That was a wonderful way to wake up."

"Glad you enjoyed it."

"Hmm, I could do the same to you."

"Yeah?" His eyes grew intense. Hot. "Are you sure—"

She put her fingers over his lips. "I want to do this."

He was still refusing to fuck her, but he wasn't going to deny her this. She threw back the covers. She wanted to see him. She started laying little kisses along his chest, circling his nipple then sucking on it lightly. He ran his fingers through her hair, gently massaging her scalp. She moaned as her body heated at his touch.

She kissed across his chest to his other nipple, giving it the same treatment. She loved listening to the way his breath hitched, how his body grew tense as she teased him. But she didn't linger long. She wanted to taste him again. She kissed her way down his stomach. There didn't seem to be an inch of fat on him. She knew his work had to be physical on the ranch. His hands were rough with calluses. And she loved them. She loved everything about him.

God, she really did love him.

Then she got lower, to where his cock was already at attention. She wrapped her hand around the base of it then took the tip of him into her mouth the way she had before.

"That's it, baby. Now lick it, run your tongue along the shaft and now lick across the head. Yes, that's it. Fuck, that feels so good."

His words filled her with confidence. She liked it when he guided her. She liked following his commands.

"Now take me into your mouth. Keep your hand around the base of me. That's it, take me in. As much as you can. Fuck yes. Your mouth is like a furnace. Christ, I'm not going to last long. That's it. Suck on me as you move back up. Fuck yes."

His breath grew faster. Sharp pants that stirred her blood. Damn, giving him pleasure was turning her on. Who knew she'd love giving blow jobs so much?

But not to just anyone. Only Bear.

She sucked on him. Drawing her mouth up then dropping it down. He groaned.

"Baby girl, the things you do to me. Never have I felt like this. Ever."

Happiness filled her. She ran her tongue along his shaft, taking him as deep as she dared then worked her way back up to the tip.

"Faster, baby. I'm close. Yes. Yes. Here I come!" He roared his release.

She took him into her mouth and swallowed his salty essence.

When he was finished, she licked him clean, lapping at him until he reached down for her and pulled her up against his chest.

"Enough, you little minx." He pressed her against his chest, running his fingers through her hair. "Damn, what am I going to do with you?"

Keep me. Please, keep me.

BEAR ANSWERED the sat phone as it rang. He moved to the front window and looked out.

She looked down at her book, trying to pretend she wasn't eavesdropping. Not that Bear was saying much.

"Yep....okay...good. Got my truck...yeah...fine."

He ended the call and she squinted down at the book, finding it hard to focus. She discreetly rubbed at her eyes, knowing if he saw her, he'd start fussing. And today she was hoping to convince him to take her virginity.

"That was my boss," he told her.

She glanced up at him. "Your boss?"

"Yep, the road has been cleared. He's coming here to us."

Her stomach dropped. She didn't want anyone else here. This place felt like it was just for them. She knew that some time it would have to end. She'd just been hoping she would have longer with him.

"He's coming here? Now?"

"Yeah. He's being overbearing as usual. He'll be here soon. Time to go home."

Her stomach dropped with dread. Home. Right. Only problem was, she was pretty certain home wasn't Aunt Rose's house.

That home was with Bear.

8

Ellie didn't quite know what to make of Clinton Jensen. Bear's boss was a hard-looking man. He had a rugged face, not what you'd call handsome but interesting all the same. But it was his manner that caught your attention and held it. She thought Bear was a gruff man. But he had nothing on this guy. Jensen had looked her over once and then dismissed her.

He stood in the center of the cabin which had seemed cozy with just the two of them, but now felt small and claustrophobic.

Bear was already moving around, tidying things up. She guessed she should be packing up her luggage, but she didn't want to. She didn't want to go. She wanted to stay here and pretend the real world didn't exist.

She wanted to stay with Bear. But she couldn't say that. He'd given her no indication he wanted anything beyond this short-term arrangement. She wished she could have a few minutes to talk to him alone. But she could hardly ask his boss to go wait in his truck. It was his cabin, after all.

She guessed at least she'd have the drive into town to talk to him. If she could just figure out what to say.

Clinton had taken his hat off after entering and now he tapped it against his thigh. He wore dark jeans, worn cowboy boots and a big, thick jacket. He didn't look like the owner of a huge ranch. For some reason she'd imagined him to be an older man. Maybe with a potbelly and a double chin. It was obvious that he didn't just sit around and direct others.

He had an air of authority about him. He wasn't the man you want to mess with, she got that straight away. Bear was wider across the shoulders and at least half a head taller and she wasn't nearly as intimidated by him as she was by Clinton Jensen.

"I brought Ike with me. Thought he could drive your truck back to the ranch and I'll take you both into town. Got to get some supplies." Jensen looked her up and down. "Unless you want me to take her on my own."

She sucked in a breath. Bear wouldn't just leave her with this stranger, would he?

"I'll go with you."

Oh, thank God. She looked at Bear, worried by how distant he was being.

"She okay to travel out in the cold?" Jensen asked Bear.

Bear looked over at her, studying her. "She should be all right if we bundle her up, she hasn't got much clothing that's suitable for this weather, though."

Clinton looked her over and she thought he probably found her lacking. "She came to Montana in winter without suitable clothing?"

"Yep," Bear answered.

Clinton just grunted. "Car's a piece of shit, too. Surprised she got as far as she did without crashing."

"It's not a piece of shit," she protested. She was getting tired of them talking about her like she wasn't even there.

"Language," both men reprimanded her.

"I was just repeating his words," she said to Bear. She didn't think it was fair she was getting told off when he was talking about her car like that.

"We're taking her to Wishingbone?" the big rancher asked.

"Russell," Bear told him. "Her aunt left her a house there." He turned to look at her for the first time in ages. "You said you had to meet the lawyer to get the key?"

"Ahh, yes, I'm meant to call her when I'm close and she'll meet me there. She was getting all the utilities turned on for me."

"All right, time's a wasting. Let's get going," Clint said brusquely.

They started moving, gathering everything up. She quickly packed up her stuff and lifted her suitcase. Clinton was walking back in as she grabbed it.

"Put that down," he barked.

She dropped it in surprise. He picked it up easily with one hand. "Little girls don't carry their own luggage."

Little girls? Had Bear told him? No, surely not. They'd only been out of her earshot for a few minutes. He carried it out the door and then Bear entered.

"Did you tell him?" she asked him as he came towards her with a large jacket.

"What?" He looked at her in confusion.

"That I've been your Little while we were here?"

"No, of course not. Why?"

"He just called me a little girl."

Bear nodded, unsurprised. "He could tell what you are. Clint's also a Daddy Dom."

He was? That surprised her. She wasn't sure she could imagine him taking care of a Little. Not like Bear had. Although he wasn't acting like her daddy now. She wished she could reach out to him for reassurance, but Clint walked back in.

"All ready to go?" Clint looked over at Bear, dismissing her again. She was starting to really dislike him.

Bear nodded. "We're ready."

It seemed like this was goodbye and she really wasn't ready for that.

THE DRIVE to Russell was done mostly in silence, other than when Ellie called her lawyer. It was the way Bear usually liked things. And he knew Clint was the same.

But he found himself missing Ellie's cheerful chatter. He longed to look back at her, to check on her, but he didn't want to make this harder on either of them. Somehow, he had to find the strength to leave her. And fuck that sucked.

"She should see a doctor," Clint said suddenly.

Bear nodded. "Yep. She's still getting headaches."

"What?" Ellie asked. "I don't need a doctor. And I'd appreciate it if the two of you didn't talk about me as though I wasn't here."

They exchanged a glance. Then Bear turned to give her a stern look. "You need to make an appointment to see a doctor, Ellie."

She gave him a stubborn look back, crossing her arms over her chest. Brat.

"We're not leaving you alone until you promise," Clint told her.

"Why do you care? You don't know me."

"You're still getting headaches, Ellie," Bear told her in a gentler voice. "You were in a car crash. You need to be checked over. If you won't agree, we'll head towards the hospital and stay there with you until you get checked out."

She stuck out her chin. "Fine. I'll go."

Bear turned back around and they all went silent once more.

Fuck, this was hard.

OKAY, she could not take the silence anymore.

She sat forward. "Umm, thanks for taking me to my aunt's house, I'm sorry to be such a bother."

Neither of them said anything. Okay, then, she guessed they liked to travel in silence. They drove along. She lasted about five minutes, but then she couldn't keep silent any longer. She was nervous and when she was nervous, she talked.

"So how far away is my aunt's house? Do you know the area? Do you think it will be hard for me to get a job?"

Clint grunted then looked over at Bear briefly.

"Not too much further to go," Bear told her. "Not sure about the job prospects, but I'm sure you'll find something."

Yeah, she wasn't so sure. Her stomach clenched tight. She was probably giving herself an ulcer with all these worries.

"I don't know what I could do. I mean, I guess I could work as a waitress. That couldn't be so hard, right? It's really beautiful out here. I've never seen this much snow."

"She always talk this much?" Clint asked Bear.

"Yep," Bear replied.

Clint grunted.

"I don't talk that much," she grumbled. "No more than a normal person. I think you two don't talk enough, what do you think of that?"

"I think that it's crazy," Clint told her.

Bear shot him a look.

"What?" Clint grumbled. "I didn't say *she* was crazy, just that talking more is a stupid idea. What's the point of talking if you have nothing to say?"

She sighed. "I just hate the silence, I guess. When it's silent I feel a little lonely." Realizing what she'd just revealed, she straightened. "Which is silly, right? All I need is some music. Let's turn the music on."

Clint cleared his throat. "The diner will be a good place to start to ask about jobs."

"Think there's a board at the community hall that also posts jobs," Bear added.

"I don't usually go into Russell, it's smaller than Wishingbone," Clint added. "But so far as I know it's safe."

"Don't hear of much crime," Bear agreed.

She hadn't exactly been asking about the crime rates, but she didn't complain. Because they were doing their best to answer her questions and put her at ease. And really, what more could a girl ask for?

"That's good to know."

"We wouldn't take you there if it was a bad area," Clint added.

She didn't know how to reply to that. How do you tell someone that you have nowhere else to go? Bad enough Bear knew how sad her life was, she didn't need Clint knowing as well.

About five minutes later, they drove past a sign welcoming them to Russell, population 764. Well, 765 now.

The nerves fluttering in her stomach grew worse. They drove through the small town. It didn't look very lively. But she guessed given the weather, it wouldn't be. At least there were still a few hours of daylight left.

Her worries over creating a life for herself here grew. They drove to the other end of town, where the houses were grander and on larger plots. Clint pulled up outside a large, two-storied house. It was an impressive building with a wrap-around porch, set well back from the road. The neighbors were barely within viewing distance.

"Are you sure this is the place?" she asked with surprise.

"That's what the mailbox says," Clint replied.

"Didn't you say the lawyer would be here?" Bear grumbled.

Almost as soon as he'd asked, a BMW pulled up in front of them and a blonde-haired woman climbed out. She was dressed warmly in a thick wool coat, gloves and a scarf. She was gorgeous and Ellie felt a bit frumpy in her worn clothes and scuffed shoes.

"Looks like that's her," Clint said as he climbed out and walked over to greet her.

Bear climbed out then opened her door. Leaning over her, he undid her seat belt and lifted her out of the truck.

"Thank you," she said quietly. Nerves made her stomach flutter.

"You okay?" he asked in a low voice.

"Sure," she said, not moving her gaze from her worn shoes. It was the first moment they'd had alone since Clint arrived at the cabin and she had to fight hard not to beg him to stay with her. To not leave her.

Put on your big girl panties, Ellie. Just because you have feelings for him doesn't mean he feels the same way. You both had a good time. Now you have to move on.

"Hey, look at me." He reached out and ran his thumb down her cheek.

She glanced up at him.

"It's going to be all right, Ellie."

"I'm afraid," she whispered.

He drew her close and she rested her head on his chest, letting the safety of his arms surround her. If only she could stay here forever. "I know you are. But you've gotten this far. If you can drive halfway across the country to an unknown place with only a few hundred dollars to your name then you can do this. I know you can."

He held her for a bit longer then pulled back. She had to bite back the urge to grab hold of him and never let go.

"Bear," she said as he turned away.

"Yeah?"

"What if I can't?" What if she couldn't do any of it? What if she was a big, fat failure just like her parents always said?

He looked down at her. Then he gave her a small smile. "Do you know that you're one of the bravest women I know?"

She snorted. "Yeah, right. I'm terrified."

"Just because you're scared doesn't mean you're not brave. Your courage comes from doing things even though you're frightened. Now you just need to see it through, to know that you can."

"Yeah. Yeah, I guess I do. Will you...can I...will I ever see you?"

He looked over at the house with a pensive look. Didn't he like the house? It looked impressive to her. Suddenly, she heard a loud cackle and frowned.

"What was that?" she asked.

"I believe it was your lawyer." He placed a hand in the small of her back and even through the huge jacket he'd given her to wear, which was apparently one of Clint's, she swore she could feel the heat of his hand.

When they walked around the truck, she saw that the lawyer had her hand on Clint's arm and was leaning into him, smiling up at him.

"Does he know her?" she asked.

"Doubt it," Bear said.

"Oh." She was confused. The woman acted like they were old friends. Ellie turned her gaze to Clint and saw the cold way he stared down at the lawyer. Okay, she'd thought him a bit abrupt and stern, but if he ever looked at her like that she'd probably run and hide.

"Hello," Ellie said, feeling the odd urge to rescue Clint.

"Hmm?" the other woman reluctantly turned her attention to Ellie and Bear. "Yes?"

"I'm Ellie Bantler. Are you Ms. George?" Ellie asked wondering if she wasn't actually the lawyer. She was here to meet Ellie, wasn't she?

"Oh yes, I am. Sorry. You didn't tell me you knew the Jensens."

There was a note of censure in the other woman's voice. As

though she thought Ellie had been trying to trick her or something.

"I don't know them. I just met Clint a few hours ago."

"Oh, right. That's okay then."

She was becoming more and more confused. Ellie turned to look at Bear who just looked impatient. "Umm, this is Bear Macall."

The other woman looked Bear up and down and nodded once then dismissed him. What a cow. She turned to Clint. "So, are you doing anything later? If not, I have a very nice bottle of cab sav at home. You could join me for a drink."

"Is she oblivious to us standing here? Or just rude?" Ellie asked Bear.

She saw his lips twitch as the other woman gasped.

"Bit of both I think," Clint replied, before extracting himself from the other woman's claws. "Maybe you should do your job and show your client her house before dark falls."

"Oh, right, yes." The other woman sent her a spiteful look. What the hell had she done? Well, she guessed that she had been a bit rude, but she was tired, cold and she needed to pee.

The other woman continued to try to draw Clint into conversation as she opened the front door then turned on the lights.

As Ellie stepped inside and started to explore the house, she managed to drown out the lawyer's voice. She moved from room to room in a daze.

"Wow," she said.

"This place is impressive," Bear commented.

She turned, not realizing he'd been behind her. They were standing in the dining room, which had a full table with eight chairs. A chandelier hung from the ceiling and there was wainscoting on the walls.

"I'll say," she said. "I've never seen a more beautiful house."

If anything, Bear grew even more closed off. She didn't understand what was going on with him. There was none of his normal warmth in his gaze. Had these last few days been an act? Did he not care about her at all? All her insecurities rushed forward. She wished he'd answered her question earlier about whether she would see him again.

"Looks like there is gas heating as well as two fire places. You'll need someone to check the chimney first before you try to light it. And then buy some firewood," Bear told her with a frown. "You got any money for that?"

"Oh, Ms. Rose left a rather substantial trust," the lawyer walked into the room, her hand still on Clint's arm. "I'm sure you'll be very pleased."

"I'd rather have my aunt than any amount of money," she snapped back.

"Huh. Of course. Yes." The other woman looked like she didn't understand a word of what Ellie had just said.

"I think we can take it from here, Ms. George" Ellie said.

"What?" the other woman said.

"Is there anything else I need to do?" Ellie tried to hold onto her patience. How had this woman ever become a lawyer?

"Well, you will need to come into my office for the details of the will and to sign some papers. Oh, and Ms. Rose had a car, it's in the garage. The key is on the same key ring for the house."

"A car. That's great." It was a huge relief to know she wouldn't be stranded here. "Anything else?"

"No, that's all." The other woman's smile dimmed as though she finally understood that she was being dismissed. But she soon rallied and turned to smile up at Clint. "Walk me out?"

She thought Clint would refuse but he gave a sharp nod, walking out with the bitch.

"Why is she acting like that when she doesn't know him?" she asked Bear.

"Because she's more interested in who he is than what he is."

"What does that mean?" she asked, confused.

"She wants him because he's rich. And because he owns the largest spread in the state."

"Seriously? That's really shallow."

"I need a shower," Clint said as he walked back in. He shuddered. "I feel dirty."

Bear rolled his eyes. "You got rid of her quick."

"As soon as she was out of Ellie's earshot, I told her exactly what I thought of her."

"Why did you wait until you were out of my earshot?" she asked.

"'Cause a little girl shouldn't have to hear those sorts of words," Clint replied.

She blushed, even though he'd spoken very matter-of-factly. As though her being a Little was, well, normal.

"We're really doing this?" he asked Bear.

Doing what? She looked over at Bear, who nodded.

Clint sighed. "I think you're making a mistake."

"You're entitled to your opinion," Bear said coolly.

"Umm, what are you guys talking about?" she asked them.

"Nothing," Bear told her.

Okay, then. She couldn't help but feel left out and a little hurt.

"I'm going to check the other rooms," she said.

"Fine. I'll be back in an hour," Clint told them both before leaving abruptly.

Bear brought in her luggage off the porch while she explored the upstairs, which was just as beautiful as downstairs. She chose a bedroom for her own, which wasn't the master as she couldn't bring herself to sleep in her aunt's bed.

She found some linens in the closet and made the bed up fresh. Bear placed her luggage in the door to the bedroom but didn't come in. Was he worried she'd jump him or something?

"Nice room. Good choice."

"Thanks," she told him. It was hard to hold back her emotions. To not ask him why he was being so distant. To beg him not to leave. Even though she loved the house, she couldn't help but wonder what she was going to do in all this space on her own.

She was in a town where she knew no one except that bitchy lawyer. And the only person she did know was acting cold and aloof. She started to sniffle.

"Hey. What's wrong?"

Bear stepped into the room and reached out for her. She shook her head and took a step back. "Sorry. I'm being silly. Just ignore me."

"Baby girl, I'm not going to ignore you when you're obviously upset. What's wrong?"

And there was her Bear. The warm, deep voice. Calling her baby. She started to sob. "Am I ever going to see you again?"

Shit. She hadn't meant to say that. She felt like a clingy idiot. It had been temporary. She'd told him she wanted nothing more. But she didn't resist as he pulled her close and rocked her.

"It's going to be all right."

"You keep saying that, but I don't know that it's true."

He rubbed her back. "I'm going to leave you with my phone number. You're going to call me if you need anything. Understand?"

"And if I do need something?"

"Then I will come."

The words calmed her. They didn't mean anything. They weren't a declaration of love, or even a promise of anything more.

But for now, they were enough.

9

"You sure you want to do this?" Clint asked as he pulled away from the curb.

"Yep." No. Every cell in his body wanted to go back to her. To hold her close. To tell her she didn't have to be scared because he would be there for her.

He rested his head back against the headrest.

"Sure about that?" Clint asked.

"Yes, I'm sure. It's for the best."

"Uh-huh, you might want to practice saying that with conviction."

He turned to glare at Clint. "It's best for her, all right? She needs to do this on her own. To know she can."

"She's a Little."

"I know that. She can still do this."

"On her own?"

"Yes, look, her parents' guilt-tripped and tricked her into quitting college and looking after them with a bunch of lies about their health. She needs time on her own. To be free."

Clint grunted. "Didn't think you were planning on locking her up."

"Taking her to the ranch would be the same thing, wouldn't it?"

"We take care of our women, they're not our prisoners."

"She's never been in a real relationship, let alone one like I would want. I gave her a taste of what it would be like, but we both agreed that it would only last while we were in the cabin. Now, it's over."

"And that's what you both want?"

"It's what we both want." God, no. It wasn't what he wanted at all. He wanted her. He loved her.

"She looked really sad for a woman who wanted to say goodbye."

Bear decided he was done talking after that. But Clint's words haunted him the whole way home.

10

She walked carefully up the slippery footpath; she'd learned the hard way just yesterday to be very careful. Her tailbone was still aching from slipping over. Shivering, she slid the key in the lock and stepped inside.

This house was beautiful. It should have brought her joy to come home to it. To step inside. This was what she wanted. She'd just been to see that bitch lawyer and she was still in a little bit of shock over the will. Aunt Rose had been so generous. She'd left her this stunning house. And a car, although she couldn't drive it since it was a manual. She'd ended up walking into town to the lawyer's office, which had been a damn cold walk. Her aunt had also left a generous trust fund.

Which she couldn't access.

Tears started to drip down her face as she walked inside and sat on the very formal sofa in the front living room. The trust fund was considerable, enough left for her to live comfortably for a while. Only problem was, she couldn't access the principal until she turned twenty-five. Until then, she would only receive the interest. Which would probably pay for the taxes and maybe heating.

She wiped at her tears. This wasn't helping. She took in a shuddering breath. "So, I need a job. That's fine. I can do this. And I could sell the car and buy an automatic."

None of that was really the reason she was sitting here crying and she knew it. She missed Bear. She missed him so much. The last two nights as she'd lain in bed, she'd held her phone and stared at his number. She'd written him into her contacts as Daddy Bear.

Except he wasn't her daddy anymore.

She let out a little sob. She wanted him. She wanted to feel his arms around her.

"Buck up, Ellie. You can do this. You can do this on your own. You don't need anyone." She took a deep breath and let it out slowly. Getting involved with Bear hadn't been a bright idea in hindsight. It had revealed parts of her she hadn't even realized she'd been keeping hidden. And now that she knew what a relationship with someone like Bear could be...hell, there was no one else like Bear. She only wanted him.

If only he felt the same way.

The doorbell ringing startled her and she moved into the foyer and opened it cautiously to find a UPS man on the other side. He held a box under one arm.

"Hello," she said.

He nodded back then held out a small electronic pad. "Sign here."

She wrote her signature and moved over to where she'd left her purse to grab a tip.

"Don't worry, ma'am. Already done," he told her cheerfully, leaving her standing in the doorway, holding the small box. She turned and shut the door, carrying it inside. No return address. Who even knew she was here? She set it on the coffee table and pulled off the tape, her heart beating rapidly as she drew out the most gorgeous teddy bear, she'd ever seen. He was fluffy and soft and wore the cutest little vest.

There was a note around his neck.

To replace Jeremiah the bear.

A sob shook her. Okay, so maybe he did care. She hugged Jeremiah and maybe she could do this. Now that she had someone with her.

BEAR KEPT CHECKING HIS PHONE. He couldn't help himself. He knew she'd gotten the bear. He'd been alerted when it had been signed for. He'd expected her to text. Not that that was the reason he'd sent it.

He just hadn't wanted her to be alone.

He finally forced himself to go eat at the dining hall, even though he didn't feel like company at the moment. Everyone was giving him a wide berth after he'd spent the last two days snapping and snarling at them all.

He couldn't help it. He'd had a few days with the woman meant for him. And then he'd had to let her go. Because she was better off without him.

When he was climbing into bed that night, his phone chimed. He glanced at it, not expecting it to be her.

Thank you for the bear. I love him.

He was surprised she texted in full sentences. But he texted back.

You are welcome.

He wasn't ready to end it there, though. With a sigh, he sent another text.

How are you?

He waited impatiently.

Good. Got a job working at the diner.

That surprised him. Hadn't the lawyer said there was a trust fund left by her aunt? But then, maybe she wasn't working for the money. Perhaps it was just to meet people. That made sense. He sent another next.

Did you meet with the lawyer? Everything okay?

Yep. All good.

He wanted to ask more but it wasn't his place.

And you have been to the doctor?

There was a longer wait now. And he started to think she wasn't going to text back. Then his screen lit up.

Not yet.

He frowned.

Little girl...

Shit. He probably shouldn't have texted that. But she knew he expected her to go to the doctor. This time five minutes passed without a reply. Finally, he couldn't wait any longer.

Do I need to come and take you?

The reply was instant this time. Part of him was disappointed. It would have given him an excuse to see her.

I feel fine.

Ellie. You need to go.

Okay. I'll make an appointment.

He could almost hear the exasperation in her voice.

Have you had any headaches?

I'm fine, Bear.

He was aware that wasn't an answer.

I better go to sleep. I start work tomorrow.

All right. Good night. Go to the doctor.

Good night.

Somehow, he felt even worse after having texted her than he had before. He longed to lay down some rules. To tell her she was coming to live with him and he didn't give a shit about her need for independence. But he wouldn't take her from one controlling relationship to another. She didn't need that. He glanced around the cabin that was his home on the ranch with a sigh. He didn't even own his own house. He didn't ever have plans to be more than he was. There was no doubt in his mind that Ellie deserved far better than him.

11

"What the hell is wrong with Bear?" Kent asked as he stormed into Clint's study.

Clint looked up with irritation. "What? You don't even knock anymore?"

"I've never fucking knocked." Kent started to pace up and down the room.

Clint sat back in his chair with a sigh. "I don't know where I went wrong. There is no respect for authority around here."

Kent shot a look. "Authority? We are in this together, brother."

"Yes, but I'm the oldest. Therefore, I should get respect."

Kent rolled his eyes. "We're not the fucking mafia."

"Sometimes I think it would be a lot simpler if we were. Then I could just shoot anyone who disagreed with me."

Kent gave him an exasperated look. He stopped pacing, resting his hands on his hips as he glared down at Clint. "Who the hell around here would disobey you?"

"Far too many people," Clint said mournfully. "I should make it a blanket rule when people are hired on, no disagreeing with the boss."

Kent snorted. "Like you're not arrogant enough as it is. You already think you're God."

"All right, so as you're already here and determined to interrupt me, so what do you mean, what is wrong with Bear?"

Kent sat in the chair across the desk from Clint. "Like you don't know. You know everything that's happening on this ranch."

Clint rubbed his hand over his face. Kent wasn't wrong. He did have a good idea what was wrong with Bear.

"It's a woman."

"A woman? When the hell did he meet a woman? Oh God, tell me he didn't join Tinder?" Kent gave him a horrified look.

It was Clint's turn to give him a look of disbelief. "How long have we known Bear? Do you seriously think he would join Tinder? I'm not even sure he knows how to use a computer."

"For fuck sake, Clint. He is not a damn dinosaur. Of course, he knows how to use a computer. He's got a phone. It's just that he never dates."

"And we both know the reason for that," Clint muttered.

"Yeah, that bitch, Maria. He's really found someone? Have you met her? Why is he in such a foul mood?"

"Because for some reason he's denying that he wants her."

"Who is it?" Kent asked.

"The woman he rescued nearly two weeks back during that snow storm. Her name is Ellie. She's a Little."

"You're kidding me?"

"I am not." When had Kent known him to joke around?

"Shit, what are the odds he'd meet a Little? Doesn't she live in Russell? Has he been to visit her?"

"Bear hasn't been off the ranch since he got back." Clint knew all the movements on and off the ranch. Yeah, he could be accused of being controlling. But he liked to protect his people. "He cares about her but for some reason he's keeping away from her. Maybe he needs a little nudge in her direction."

Kent sighed. "Poor Bear."

"What are you talking about?"

"You're about to interfere."

"Well, isn't that why you came to me? So, I could fix him?" Clint demanded.

"Don't try to pretend with me, you were dying to interfere. It's what you live for. Bear won't be happy, though."

Clint shrugged. "God doesn't worry about whether people get pissed off or not."

Ken rolled his eyes as he stood. "I suppose it's pointless of me to point out that you're not actually God."

"Around here I am."

"So, when are you going after the girl?"

Bear groaned as Clint walked up behind him.

"I'm headed home," he told him as he trudged towards his cabin. He'd had his dinner. He was tired. He wanted to go to bed, not be interrogated by his boss.

"I'll walk with you."

Bear shot him a glance.

"Cold out tonight," Clint remarked.

"It's cold most nights." What did Clint want? He never talked about the weather.

"Hope that girl of yours is keeping herself warm."

"Not my girl." So that was his plan. He was here to talk about Ellie. Bear hadn't heard from her since that night she'd texted him when she'd received the teddy bear. That was nearly a week ago. He'd wanted to text her so many times but he'd held himself back.

She was busy building a life. Without him.

"But you want her to be, don't you?" Clint asked.

"What I want has nothing to do with it."

"I'm surprised you haven't been in to check on her."

He sighed and turned to Clint. "What do you want from me?"

"I want to know why you just left her there? It was obvious there was something between the two of you. And you just walked away and left her on her own."

"It's what she wanted."

"What she wants isn't necessarily what she needs."

"Jesus, just because you're a nosy bastard who likes to control everything around you, doesn't mean you get to interfere in my life." He glared at Clint. He wasn't pulling this shit on him.

"You're not usually this grumpy."

"You mean I normally ignore you when you get like this," Bear said to him. "But I don't want or need your interference, Clint."

"Doesn't mean you're not going to get it."

Bear let out a huge sigh. "Why do you have to be like this?"

"I just want to help."

"Well, don't. I told you about her life with her parents. She wants some time to herself. Some independence. She doesn't want another controlling relationship."

"Come on, you'd hardly treat her like her parents did. She was their slave. She'd be your Little. Your sub."

"It's not what she wants," he gritted out between his teeth.

"Did you ask her?"

He ran his hand over his face. "Look, she needs this time to herself and when she's ready for a relationship, well, she deserves someone better than me."

"Jesus, I knew it would be some bullshit like that," Clint muttered.

"It's not bullshit. Did you see that house? And you heard the lawyer, she's rich. What the fuck can I offer her?"

Clint crossed his arms over his chest, giving Bear a look of disapproval. "This is all about Maria, because she used you to get to me. She was a gold-digging bitch."

"I know that."

"You think Ellie is like her?"

"Of course, she isn't," he yelled. Then he took a calming breath. "Ellie is kind and sweet and honest. Doesn't mean I have anything to offer her."

"Except a man who will love and take care of her. Put her first. Treat her how she deserves to be treated. Cherish her for who she is. If she gets into a relationship with the wrong person, they will use her, walk all over her."

He clenched his hands into fists, hating the thought of his Ellie with someone like that.

"Just stay out of my business, Clint." He turned and stormed away. He'd done the right thing. He had.

He just wished he fully believed that.

SHE TRUDGED HER WAY HOME, trying to avoid the icy patches. It was growing darker and even though the streetlights were on, she wished she'd brought a torch. She'd thought once it stopped snowing that it would get warmer, but she was sadly mistaken. At least her house was nice and warm. She'd had all these ideas of what her life would be like once she left her parents' house. Only, nothing was working out like she thought. The house she'd thought would be a haven felt scary and overwhelming.

The people in the town were nice, but she hadn't met anyone she might make friends with. They all seemed to be in their own groups and she was left on the sidelines. She felt lost. And more alone than ever.

And it was all Bear's fault.

He'd shown her what life could be like with someone who cared about her. Or who she thought had cared. But he hadn't texted her except for that one night. And when he'd started to boss her around, she'd thought...well, she'd hoped...yeah, she was stupid. She'd thought that he would check back to see if she'd followed his order to see the doctor. So, she hadn't gone in the hopes that he'd come storming in and ...what? Spank her? Fuck her?

Both, please.

What an idiot she was. He hadn't checked in on her again. He didn't care. And she was on her own.

She kept her head down as she walked, concentrating on putting one foot in front of the other. She still hadn't bought a new car so she was stuck walking everywhere. She needed to get a winter coat, but the shops in the small town were far too expensive, so she was stuck wearing the one Clint had left her. Which she was grateful for. But it was huge and at some stage she needed to return it to him.

She wasn't concentrating on her surroundings so she didn't see the truck outside her house. She should have, of course. But she blamed her inattention on tiredness. She wasn't sleeping well. She spent most nights huddled under the covers with her new teddy bear, who she'd named Jeremiah Bear Junior.

She missed Bear so much.

"Do you always walk around without paying attention to your surroundings, little girl?" a deep voice asked.

With a startled gasp, she looked up to see Clint scowling at her. He was leaning against his truck, his arms were crossed over his wide chest, he had a cowboy hat secured firmly on his head, and he was wrapped up in a warm jacket.

She took a step back. Even though she knew Clint, she couldn't help but feel a bit intimidated, especially since he was glaring at her disapprovingly.

She gasped in a breath, her hand to her chest. "What are you doing? You gave me a fright."

"I was standing here for five minutes, watching you walk up

the path. You didn't look up once. You didn't watch your surroundings. Anyone could have snuck up on you and hurt you."

She looked at him in alarm. "Is that what you're here to do?"

His eyes widened, his arms dropping to his sides as he gaped at her. "Of course, I'm not."

"Why are you here then? Is it for your jacket?" She started to take it off.

"Leave that on, little girl. It's too cold to be stripping off. Especially for a little thing like you. I'm not here for the jacket. You can keep it."

"I was going to give it back," she said defensively.

"What are you doing walking around in the dark in this sort of weather?"

"It's not late. I've just finished a shift at the diner. I've got a job now."

"Yeah, Bear told me."

"He talks to you about me? How is he? Is he doing okay?" She wished she hadn't said anything when his eyes narrowed slightly. She should have acted disinterested. Shoot.

"Where is your car? You shouldn't be walking when it's nearly dark. You could slip and hurt yourself."

She frowned at him. Had he forgotten already? But this didn't seem the type of man who forgot things easily. "I crashed it, remember?"

"Yes, I remember," he said impatiently. "I also remember the lawyer saying your aunt left you a car."

"Oh yeah." She'd forgotten he'd been there then. "It's a manual transmission. I can't drive it. I never learned how."

"So, you've been walking everywhere?"

"Keeps me fit," she said lightly.

"Did you tell Bear this?" he demanded.

"Nothing to do with Bear. And it's nothing to do with you. If you came here just to grill me about my transportation options, then you can just go." She was being rude, she knew. But she just wasn't up to talking to him. Seeing him made her miss Bear even more. Tears pricked at her eyes and she was determined not to give into them. She tried to walk past him, but he stepped forward and reached out to grab hold of her arm.

"Wait just a minute, little girl. I'm not done talking and I didn't dismiss you."

Her eyes widened as she gaped up at him. She wasn't sure whether to be horrified at his arrogance or impressed. "First of all, stop calling me little girl. I'm not a little girl. I'm a grown woman. And secondly, dismiss me? Really? I'm not some schoolgirl, and you're not the principal."

"Hell no. I'm not. Thank God. I'm not after a schoolgirl. And I don't want to be murdered by Bear."

She didn't know what on earth he was talking about. Why would Bear get angry with him? "What are you doing here, Clint? Does Bear know you're here?"

"Of course, he doesn't. I'm here because I wanted to check up on you. Didn't feel right just leaving you here. I know Bear would have been here himself but..."

"But what?"

"He thinks he's not good enough for you."

"What?" She gaped at him. "Not good enough for me? Why would he think that?"

"Can I come inside? Got a story to tell you and I'd rather we were inside in the warmth."

"Oh, ahh, sure, come in." Any nervousness she felt around him died when he said he had something to tell her about Bear.

He followed her inside as she moved back towards the kitchen. "Want some hot chocolate?"

"Got marshmallows?"

"Well, you brought my groceries, so you know I do." She gave him a chiding look. That's what he'd gone away to do for an hour while she and Bear had been unpacking. "I'm still going to pay you back."

"You try and you'll be in big trouble," he warned. "They were a housewarming gift."

God, he was so stubborn.

"Thank you for doing that."

He waved off her gratitude, looking uncomfortable.

She sighed. He was impossible. Arrogant. Infuriating. And given to generous acts of kindness that obviously made him uncomfortable.

Clint just watched as she made them both a hot drink. They sat across from each other at the small table in the kitchen.

"Why does Bear think he's not good enough for me? Bear's the best person I know."

He nodded. "He is. And I'm glad you see that. He's honest. Smart. A hard worker. Loyal. He'd make a good daddy."

She blushed. "I don't want to talk about that."

He gave her a knowing look. "But he's got one flaw. He has a bit of a self-esteem issue when it comes to women. See, there was this woman a while back. Her name was Maria. He met her in a bar. He doesn't go out much, but she was gorgeous and pretended to be sweet and submissive."

"What happened to her?"

"They started dating. She lived in Wishingbone, and she kept pressing him to take her to the ranch. So, a few weeks into the relationship he took her out there."

"And?"

"And turns out the only reason she sank her hooks into Bear was to get to me. She was all over me as soon as she got through those gates."

"Oh no, poor Bear. Why would she want you over him?"

"Ouch." He rubbed his chest. "That was a direct blow."

"Oh, sorry, I didn't mean...it's just..." She blushed, feeling awful.

He winked at her. "It's okay, sweetheart. It's a good thing that you like him. It's what he needs. Someone who thinks the sun rises and falls on him. Someone who will be loyal to him. Maria really did a number on his ability to trust. You're the first woman he's shown any interest in in a long time. So, you can understand why I feel protective of him. I don't want him hurt again."

"I bet he really appreciates that," she said dryly.

"Funnily enough, he doesn't. No one on the ranch appreciates what I do for them."

She rolled her eyes. "You poor baby. So now you're here to decide if I'm good enough for your friend?"

Perhaps she should have been offended by that. But actually, she thought it was nice that Bear had someone looking out for him. Made her wish she had the same.

"I really miss him," she confessed, looking down at her hot chocolate.

"He misses you too, little girl. But you're going to have to be the one to go to him. I saw the way you two looked at each other. He's been in a right mood this past week. How you been doing without him?"

Bear had been missing her? Really? "Are you sure he's missing me? Maybe he's upset for another reason?"

"Nope. I've known that man all my life, nothing much upsets him. But he's been in a hell of a mood since we left you here. Now answer my question."

Jesus, he was demanding. What had been his question? Oh, yeah, how had she been without Bear. That was easy. "I've been miserable."

He nodded. "Good."

"Well, thanks, glad you think my misery is a good thing." He really was a strange man.

"It is if it means you care about him."

"I do." More than he could possibly know.

"And you'd give this up to come live at the ranch with him?" He waved his hand around at the house.

"In a heartbeat." This was a lovely house, but it wasn't home. That was with Bear.

"That's what I like to hear."

"But how does this change anything? How will I convince him that I want him? We're not even talking."

"Leave that up to me." He studied her for a moment. "You look exhausted. You haven't been sleeping?"

She shrugged. "Not really."

"You been to see a doctor and have him check you over?"

She stared down at the countertop. He sighed. "I'm going to take that as a no. Bear know that?"

"No."

"So, you broke your promise to him." His voice had a dark note of disapproval in it. She shivered slightly. "You knew what you were supposed to do and you broke the rules. And that might just be what we need to get him here."

"What?" She could not figure this guy out.

"Go upstairs and have a shower and get into your pajamas," he told her.

"Are you always this bossy?"

"Yes. And until Bear takes responsibility for you again, you're my responsibility."

"Why?" she asked.

He sighed. "Because Bear is my best friend. I want him to be happy. I came here for him. But now that I've seen you, walking around in threadbare shoes, in a borrowed jacket that is far too big for you and with big black marks under your eyes, I can see that you need him even more than he needs you. You're lost, aren't you, little girl?"

"I'm not lost. I'm fine." She really wasn't though.

"Don't lie to me. That's the last warning you get."

She knew she shouldn't ask. She told herself not to ask. "Or what?"

"Or I tell on you to Bear."

She rubbed at her forehead. The headache had been brewing for hours, which wasn't a good sign. But now she was seeing spots in her vision and her stomach was starting to bubble with nausea. She'd only taken a few sips of the hot chocolate.

Clint watched her closely. "You have a headache?"

"Yeah, and his name is Clinton Jensen."

He snorted. "It's not the first time I've heard that."

"That's not a surprise to me."

He gave a speculative look. Then he nodded as though he'd made up his mind about something.

"Do you really think he wants me?" she whispered. She was so scared to take a chance. To believe what Clint said. Because she wasn't sure she could stand for Bear to reject her.

Clint reached over and grabbed hold of her cold hand in his large one. "He does. Now, don't worry, I'm going to fix things."

She shook her head. "It's not that easy. You can't fix things for other people."

"Yeah, I can. Don't you worry now. Go get into your pajamas. I won't ask a third time."

Bossy bastard. She glared at him, but found herself standing and heading towards the stairs.

She didn't know why she felt compelled to do as he ordered. She should probably kick him out of her house. She went upstairs and got ready for bed. Her head was really aching and her pain relief was in her handbag downstairs. Dressed in a pair of old pajamas that had seen better days, she went back downstairs and grabbed her bag off the hall table. She pulled the bottle of pills out, shaking out a couple onto her hand.

A big hand reached over her shoulder and grabbed the bottle. He held them up. "I thought I asked you if you had a headache?"

She placed her hand over her stomach as it clenched violently. "I'm gonna be sick."

He swept her up into his arms and ran for the bathroom. He got there just in time, holding her over the toilet as she heaved and heaved. Tears dripped down her face and she sobbed, agony engulfing her. When she was finished vomiting, her head felt like there were shards of glass tearing their way into her skull and her stomach rolled sickeningly.

"Sweetheart, it's okay. I have you. You're okay."

She wished she could sink into his words. And the arms that were holding her. But they were the wrong arms and the wrong voice.

"I want Bear."

"I know you do, little one," Clint said in a soft voice.

"I'm sorry I just vomited in front of you." God, this was embarrassing. "Please let me have the painkillers. My head is so sore."

"It's a migraine?" he asked.

"Yes."

"Okay. Did you get these before your accident?"

"No." She was incapable of speaking more than one-word sentences it seemed. In fact, she didn't really want to speak at all.

He gently pulled her up into his arms. She didn't know where he was taking her. She just hoped it was somewhere dark and calm and soothing. Where she could lick her wounds. As if he'd read her mind, he laid her down on her bed. Yes. Thank goodness. Blankets were settled over her. And then something cool was placed over her eyes. She let out a low whimper.

"Just leave that there, sweetheart. Rest. It's all going to be okay. I promise."

She wasn't sure what he meant by that. But right at this moment, she no longer cared.

12

Bear was in a foul mood. Then again, when wasn't he in a foul mood at the moment? He wasn't really fit to be around other people. He stomped into his cabin. He knew he should head to the dining hall and get some dinner, but he didn't feel like eating. He looked longingly over at the bottle of whiskey. Except he'd been drinking too much of that lately, and he wasn't a man who liked to lose control.

He needed to get himself back to that place where he'd been. Before Ellie. When he hadn't been this rioting mess of emotions.

Maria's betrayal had hurt, but it had nothing on the pain of losing Ellie.

He sat on the sofa in his cabin with a sigh and stared down at the phone in his hand. Maybe he should text her. Check on her. Make sure she'd been to the doctor. But what if she hadn't been? Then he'd have to follow through on his threat to take her. Seeing her again probably wasn't in his best interests right now.

His phone rang and he thought about ignoring it. But with a sigh, he looked at the screen and saw Clint's name. Great. Maybe he'd have a job for him to do. Something to take his mind of Ellie.

"Yeah," he barked down the phone.

"Well, that's a cheerful greeting."

"What do you want, Clint?"

"You know, I am still your boss." There was no anger in the other man's voice. He was baiting him.

"So, you just called me up to fire me, is that it?" Maybe an argument with Clint would ease some of his tension.

"Of course, I didn't damn well call you to fire you. Jeez, touchy much? I'm at Ellie's house."

It was like a bucket of cold water over his head. Thoughts of Maria came screaming back and he shook them off. Clint had never done anything to lead Maria on. She'd come onto him. He trusted Clint. Even though they both had similar taste in women, Clint would never go after someone who meant something to him. Still he couldn't help a surge of jealousy. "What the hell are you doing at *my* Ellie's house?"

"Whoa. Calm down. It's not like that. I'm here to help you."

He rubbed his forehead. It wasn't the first time that one of Clint's plans had given him a headache. Or backfired on them all. "Please tell me you didn't go there in order to get her to see me. Please tell me you didn't interfere in my life like that. Because you know if you did, I'm going to have to hurt you."

"I expect you'll forgive me once Ellie's in your bed. Or over your knee. That girl needs a good spanking."

He clenched his free hand then forced himself to relax. Clint was just trying to goad him.

"Why are you at Ellie's house? And where is Ellie?"

"Well, I've just put her to bed."

That surge of jealousy came through once more. "Are you fucking kidding me? Are you trying to get yourself killed?"

"You know, I'm not used to you threatening to kill me twice in one conversation. You certainly weren't this mad when I revealed what Maria was. Makes me think she wasn't really important to you. At least not as important as this girl."

Nothing was more important to him than Ellie. Her happiness. That was what came first. Even before his own.

"Clint, stop fucking around and just tell me what's going on. Why did you have to put Ellie to bed?"

"Because she just vomited everywhere and she was worn out."

"She's sick?" His heart beat rapidly. He had stood and headed towards the door before he even realized what he planned to do. He put on his boots with one hand and reached for his truck keys.

"Migraine by the looks of it," Clint said. This time he had a note of concern in his voice. "And I would say this isn't the first time she's had one. Don't know if she had them before the concussion or not, but she needs to get them checked out."

"She promised she would go to the doctor."

"But that doesn't mean she did."

Bear paused took a deep breath. "She never went to the doctor?"

"Nope. Like I told you, she needs a good spanking. She tell you that she can't access that trust fund yet?"

What? What was she living on?

"We haven't really been talking. She did say she had a job. I thought it was to meet people."

"Oh yes, her job. The one she has to walk to because her aunt's car is a stick and she can't drive it. Not sure if she had insurance on that other piece of crap she was driving. Oh, and my jacket is the only piece of decent clothing she has."

Shit. Shit. Shit. He climbed into his truck and started it up.

"I thought she was taken care of. She had a nice house, a trust fund, a car."

"Yeah, well, sometimes it's not stuff that a person needs."

This was his fault? Of course, it was. He'd left her. The call switched over to Bluetooth and he put his phone down and started down the driveway.

"Of course, she should have told you all this. You did tell her to contact you if she needed anything or was in trouble."

He had.

"She was walking along the road, not paying any attention to her surroundings. Anyone could have walked up to her and hurt her."

"I should never have left her." He punched his fist against the steering wheel, feeling sick to his stomach. "Have you called the doctor?"

"I rang Doc and he said the best thing for her was just to sleep it off in a dark room with silence. I told her about Maria."

Fuck. This was why Clint shouldn't be allowed off the ranch. "Well, you're just stacking up the friendship points today, aren't you?"

"I just thought I should come here and check on her. I feel responsible for her too."

"You went to interfere. Maybe see if you could do a bit of matchmaking."

"Hey, if the ranch ever goes under at least I'll have a second career choice to fall back on."

"Yeah, I'll buy a domain name for you now. Interferingbastard.com."

"Hope my customers are more appreciative than you."

13

Her mouth was so dry. Ick and when she swallowed all she could taste was vomit.

Slowly, she rolled over. She felt like she been run over by a truck. Her whole body ached. Even her tongue felt gross. She attempted to pull herself up. She needed a drink. And a tranquilizer.

"Easy, baby girl," a low, raspy voice said. "Let me get you what you need. You just lie there."

She recognized the voice, but she still wasn't sure whether she was actually awake. "So, I'm still dreaming, then?"

She opened her eyes and looked up. She couldn't see much since the room was so dark.

"You're not dreaming, Ellie. Well, unless you think you're in a nightmare," he teased.

"Not a nightmare. Not unless you're going to leave again."

He sighed. "Do you think I can turn on the light without causing you any pain?"

She moved her head slowly from side to side. "I think so, if I adjust my eyes slowly." She put her arm over her eyes as he switched on the bedside lamp. Then she moved her arm carefully away and blinked, opening her eyes slowly. She looked up into Bear's concerned face. God, she'd missed him.

"Can I have a drink?" she asked in a croaky voice.

He immediately reached for the glass on the bedside table. It had a straw in it which he held to her lips. Huh, whoever knew she'd kind of miss the sippy cup.

"You're always having to take care of me."

He smiled. "I enjoy it. How are you feeling?" He gave her a concerned look.

"I'm all right. Migraine is gone. I just feel exhausted. You look tired." There were dark crescents under his eyes.

"I haven't been sleeping," he admitted. "Not since the night I left you here." He reached out and grabbed hold of her hand, running his thumb over the back of her hand.

"Clint called you?" she guessed.

"Yep."

"You came because I was sick?" She wished it was because he'd missed her so much, he couldn't be without her.

He studied her for a moment. "That's part of the reason. When he called me, I jumped straight in my truck and drove here. I was worried about you the entire drive. But I was also happy."

"Happy?" That seemed a weird reaction to her being ill.

"Because I was going to see you again. I've missed you, Ellie."

Tears dripped down her cheeks. He reached up and wiped them away. "Hey, shh, don't cry."

"I've missed you too. I know this is what I said I wanted. To be on my own. To be my own boss. But it's been awful. This house is huge and it gets scary at night. And I'm so lonely. I miss you. I miss you so much."

"It's okay. I'm here now, baby girl. I'm not going anywhere." He ran his fingers through her hair, his touch a comfort she had desperately missed.

"You promise?"

"I promise. I made a mistake leaving you. I wanted to give you space. To give you what you wanted, the chance to be alone. I didn't want you to go from one controlling relationship to another."

She frowned. "What do you mean? What controlling relationship? You mean like what my parents did to me? Bear, you could never be like that."

He shrugged his shoulders. "No, not like that. But what I want isn't exactly normal."

"Maybe not. But I like what you want. In fact, I think I need it."

"I didn't want you to resent me or to wonder what your life would have been like if you'd had a chance to live on your own. And I guess that part of me thought you deserved better than me."

"Better than you? There is no one better than you." He was the best man she'd ever met. Hands down.

He gave her a small smile. "I'm just a simple man, honey. I live a simple life. And you have all this."

He swept his hand around.

"What do you mean? This house? Bear, this is a gorgeous house but it's not a home. A home is with the people you love, right? And I love you."

He grew still. "You do?"

She sucked in a breath. She knew it would decimate her if he didn't feel the same but she had to tell him. "Yes, I love you, Bear."

He leaned in and kissed her lightly. "That's good. Since I love you more than I ever thought was possible."

Happiness filled her, making her feel a little lightheaded. Then she started to wonder about what exactly that meant for them. "What happens now? Where do we go from here?"

"That depends on you, baby girl. You can stay living here. I won't be able to see you every day because of my job, but you can be damn sure that I will be calling and texting often. You tend to get into trouble when you're unsupervised."

Trouble? What trouble? "I do not!"

"Uh-huh. You told me twice that you would go to the doctor." He gave her a disapproving look.

"Oh, that." She bit her lip.

"Yes, that."

She squirmed slightly then winced as her body protested the movement. "I didn't have much money and I've just started working at the diner and I..."

"Yes?"

"I guess maybe I was hoping you would text me to check that I'd been and then when you found out I hadn't been you would come to see me." It was humiliating to admit and when she looked up into his face, he looked just as stern as before.

"So, you were trying to manipulate me?"

"No! Well, maybe a little bit. I just wanted to see you." Okay, so the plan was a little juvenile.

"And you didn't think to just ask me to come see you?" he asked.

That would have been the mature way to handle things. But she'd felt so unsure of herself, of him and she guessed she hadn't been brave enough to try. "I'm sorry. It was a silly way to handle things, but I just wasn't sure what your response would be."

He sighed. "We're a pair of idiots."

She gave him a hopeful look. "Does that mean you won't punish me for not going to the doctor?"

"Oh, no, you're getting your butt roasted. After the doctor has given the okay, that is. I won't ever be lenient with you when it comes to your health, little girl."

She stared at him in horror. "You're not going to ask him if you can spank me, will you?"

He grinned. "We have our own doctor out at the ranch. He

won't bat an eyelid over me asking that." He grew sober. "I hope I didn't bring these migraines on when I spanked you at the cabin."

"You didn't bring them on. To be honest, I'm not sure what triggers them. I'm also having a little problem with my vision."

He glared down at her. "Little girl, you are in such trouble. What problems?"

She shrugged. "When I try to read, the words tend to dance around a bit, maybe it's because of the concussion?"

He muttered something under his breath.

"Umm, Bear?" she interrupted.

He took a deep breath in as though to calm himself. "Yes, baby?"

She played nervously with the covers. He loves you. Be brave. "What if I don't want to live here? What if I didn't want to just see you on the weekends?"

He looked thoughtful. "You saying you want to live with me?"

She sighed. Good, he understood. "Yes, please. I mean, if you want me to, that is. I can stay here if you don't." She bit at her lip worriedly. He reached out and pulled her lower lip free of her teeth. He rubbed it soothingly. Well, it was probably meant to be soothing, but it shot sparks of arousal at her clit.

"Baby girl, there's nothing I want more than to have you with me. All the time. But are you sure you want that? I would be more than just your boyfriend. I'd also be your daddy, your Dom."

She tried to pull herself up into a seated position. He ended up having to help her, arranging the pillows behind her so she could sit up comfortably. She was so tired.

"Bear, I know you're worried that I'll think you are controlling me like my parents. But I don't see things that way at all. Because you are the opposite of them. You always put me first. You take care of me. You love me. And this sort of relationship is what I want as well. I've never felt safer than I did during those few days with you. That's what I want. To be your Little girl. And to be your woman."

"I want your promise if it ever gets too much or you find you don't want to live in that sort of relationship anymore that you will tell me. Straight away."

"It won't," she said quickly.

He gave her a stern look.

"But I will," she added.

"Promise. And this time, I want you to keep your promise."

She held out her pinky finger. "Pinky promise. I can never break a pinky promise."

He rolled his eyes. But curled his pinky finger with hers. "I guess I should have made you pinky promise to go to the doctor."

She grimaced. "Are you sure we can't just wipe the slate clean and start again?"

"I don't suppose we can," he told her in a dry voice.

"Yeah, that's what I was afraid you were going to say."

He ran a finger over her cheek. "I'll always put your health first, baby girl. I'm so glad that I found you that day. Because now you'll be mine forever."

"So, I'm coming back to the ranch to live with you?" she asked in a hopeful voice.

"There is nothing I want more." He kissed her gently then sat back. "But there are things I haven't told you about the ranch. Things about the way we live there."

"Like Clint thinks he's God and he gets to interfere in everybody's relationships?"

He grinned. "Oh good. So, you already know about the worst of it."

"Is he still here?"

Bear shook his head. "No. Clint is a work-a-holic. He hardly ever takes time off. You should probably be flattered that he took the time to come out and check on you himself."

"Oh yeah, I'll get right onto that right now."

"On the ranch, Clint's word is law. He can be an interfering bastard. But he really does want to take care of those he considers his. His great-great-grandfather started that ranch. He wanted a safe place to live with his wife, and her other husband."

Her eyes widened. "She had two husbands?"

"Yep. And he only allowed like-minded people onto the ranch. Others who believed that men should be head of the household, which wasn't such an odd thing back then, but they wanted a safe place for women to live. Women have always been cherished and protected on Sanctuary. And the men take all the responsibility. Make all the rules. And put their women over their knees when those rules aren't followed."

She gaped at him. "Wow. All the women on the ranch live like that?"

"Yep. More than that, they want it. Enjoy it. Although, to be honest, there aren't that many women living there currently. Every woman has to have a guardian. And the only woman who isn't married is Clint's sister."

"A guardian?"

He nodded. "Someone who watches over her, takes responsibility for her and punishes her if necessary. Usually guardians are their husbands or boyfriends, but sometimes it's a family member like with Clint's sister."

"But what if a guardian abused one of them? Was horrible to them?"

He reached forward and took her hands in his, rubbing them. "Do you ever believe that I would abuse my power over you?"

"Of course, I don't." She clung to his hands. "But you're you, Bear. You've got more integrity in your little finger than most people have in their whole bodies."

He flushed, looking embarrassed. That was pretty damn adorable.

"But I know that other people aren't like that," she worried.

"Okay, I have another question. Do you think that Clint would allow anyone onto his ranch who was even the slightest bit abusive to a woman? That I would? Everyone on that ranch is there because they believe women should be kept safe. We would never allow any abuse."

She thought that through. "Clint would know, wouldn't he?"

"Everyone would know. And it would not go well for any man who ever abused a woman. If for some reason I lost my mind and hurt you, then you go straight to Clint and you tell him. And you'll be taken care of. And you'll never have to see me again."

"You'd never do that."

"I know. But if I did, you would go to him," he told her in a commanding voice.

"But he's your friend. I'd be the one who'd be sent away."

He shook his head. "You still don't get it, baby. Women come first. Always. We don't give them rules to be assholes. Or because we enjoy spanking them."

"You don't?" she asked cheekily.

"Well, I don't necessarily like causing you pain. But a sexy spanking could be fun."

Her body heated at his words. "Yeah. I think that's the only spankings I'm going to get from now on."

He gave a bark of laughter. "I wouldn't bet on that."

She wrinkled her nose at him. "You'll see. I'll be a good little girl from now on."

"We will see. You're still very pale. Ellie, I love you so much. I can't stand the idea of you being in pain and not telling me. We'll get Doc to examine you as soon as we get back to the ranch. Hopefully, he can figure out what these headaches are about."

"Are any of the other women on the ranch like me? A Little?"

He looked thoughtful. "No, I don't think so. Although sometimes Clint's sister can act a bit like a teenager. But that doesn't mean anyone will make fun of you or look down on you."

"I don't feel comfortable showing my Little side to anyone else."

"Then you don't have to," he said easily. "It will just be special for the two of us."

She smiled up at him. "I like the sound of that."

"Like I said, everything is different for everyone. And we'll do what's right for us."

She held up her arms and he carefully pulled her into his lap, holding her close. "I love you, Daddy."

"I love you too, baby girl."

"So, does this mean I get to know what your real name is?" she asked hopefully.

"Not a chance."

14

"I can't believe you actually asked him about spanking me," Ellie said to Bear as soon as they walked into his cabin on the ranch.

"I told you I was going to."

"Yeah, but I thought you were joking about that."

They'd spent the night after her migraine at her Aunt Rose's house then the next morning, he'd packed up all her stuff, without letting her lift a finger, and driven her out here. She'd decided that she might rent Aunt Rose's house out. It deserved to have a family living in it.

The ranch was beautiful. She was pretty certain it was heaven on earth, nestled between two mountains and surrounded on two sides by trees that seemed to go on forever.

Bear had spent yesterday settling her in and then this morning, he'd taken her to see Doc. Who had to have the worst bedside manner of any doctor she'd ever met.

But he had some good news. He'd given her an eye test and discovered she was far-sighted. He believed that was causing her headaches and blurry vision. She would need to go to an optometrist, and get some glasses, of course. But he was hopeful once she did that the migraines would clear up.

When Bear, the rat, had asked him if it was safe to spank her, he'd told him to lay off any heavy punishments for a bit. Until they'd made sure that the headaches were entirely related to her eyesight. But he'd added that a few swats would be all right.

Those were his exact words. Her cheeks were still burning in mortification. Then Bear had gone and asked if it was all right for them to have sex. Doc had been very matter-of-fact when he'd replied that as long as he wasn't going to tie her upside down or do anything else extreme to fuck her, they were good.

"I'm so embarrassed."

"There's no reason to be. Neither Doc nor I were. If I'm going to look after you then I need to know your limitations, don't I? I don't want to do anything that will harm you."

"I know...but...sheesh..." She sat on the bed and stared at her feet.

He crouched down in front of her and lifted her chin so she had to look at him. "I'm sorry you were embarrassed, baby girl. But I can't let that get in the way of taking care of you, okay?"

"Okay. I...umm...I suppose you have to get back to work now." She looked from him to the bed.

"Actually, I'm off until tomorrow. What would you like to do for the rest of the day?" He gave her a knowing look.

"Well, I suppose we have been given the green light to...well... and..." She blew out a frustrated breath. "I wish I was sophisticated and worldly and could talk about this stuff."

He chuckled and stood. For a moment she worried he was going to leave. But he just started undoing his shirt buttons. "Well, I for one, am glad you're not sophisticated and worldly. I like you just the way you are."

By now, he had his shirt off and her gaze was caught on his chest. All that gorgeous muscle encased in tanned skin and he was hers. All hers. Her mouth went dry, nerves fluttered in her stomach. Were they really doing this?

She reached up and ran her hands over his chest, down his stomach until she reached his belt. She slipped it open then undid his jeans, pulling them down over his ass.

His cock was straining against his black boxer shorts and she leaned in and licked it right through the cloth.

He groaned as she ran her tongue up and down the length.

"Enough. Take him out."

"Him, huh?"

"Well he's certainly not a she. Stop teasing me, minx. I want to feel your mouth on me."

She gently tugged at his boxers, but he obviously grew impatient because he took over, dragging them down along with his jeans and chucking them to one side. She leaned forward and grasped hold of his shaft at the base and licked along the head, then sucked him into her mouth.

"Fuck, baby. Feels so good."

She hummed in pleasure as she licked her way up the shaft then took him into her mouth again, sucking on him strongly. She reached out with her free hand and cupped his balls.

"Oh hell. You do not know how amazing that feels. Your mouth is a furnace around my cock. Take me deep, honey."

She took him down, loving that she could do this for him, bring him such pleasure.

"Faster, baby. That's it. Suck me inside you. Oh fuck, yes." She heard the need in his voice. Knew he was close.

"I'm going to come. Suck me down. Such a good girl to swallow. Yes, that's it. Christ!"

When he was finished, she licked him clean then leaned back to smile up at him. "Okay?"

His gaze was hot. Intense. "Okay doesn't even cover it. Come here." He crooked a finger at her and she stood. He immediately picked her up. She wrapped her legs around his waist as he kissed her, not seeming to care that she still had his taste in her mouth. Then he laid her back on the bed and stripped her. He tugged off her leggings and the thick socks that he'd given her to wear, which were about five sizes too big since they were his.

Then he reached for her sweater, gently tugging it off.

"You have entirely too much clothing on. You should spend all of your time naked," he grumbled

"That could be rather cold," she commented as he removed her thermal shirt. He'd insisted on buying her some warmer clothes yesterday before they'd headed to the ranch. "We'd have to move to Hawaii for that to be possible."

"It's a thought," he muttered. She knew he wasn't serious. He loved it here. The mountains and quiet suited him.

She wasn't wearing a bra and in no time, she was lying there naked while his hot gaze devoured her.

"Beautiful." He ran a finger between her breasts then up over her right nipple. She trembled. She was so turned-on she didn't think it was going to take much to push her over the edge.

"Did you masturbate while we were apart?" he asked as he moved his finger over her nipple.

What? Why did he do this to her? "Bear, you can't ask me that."

He lay alongside her and ran his finger down her stomach to the very top of her pussy then just as he was about to reach the top of her slit, he changed direction and moved his finger back up towards her breast.

"I just did. And you're going to answer me. If it makes you feel any better, I masturbated every night. And while I was rubbing one off, I was thinking about you naked. About the taste of this sweet pussy." He cupped her mound. "The little sounds of pleasure you make as your pleasure grows. The way you tense up then explode, your entire body shaking when you come.

He pushed his finger partially up inside her. "Do you want me here tonight, Ellie? Do you want me to take your virginity?"

He thrust his finger in and out of her. Her heart raced. It wasn't nearly enough. She needed him. Felt so empty. So needy.

"Yes," she told him breathlessly.

He pulled his finger out, it glistened with her juices. He ran it over her nipple, coating the tight nub with her dew. "Then answer me."

He leaned in and licked her essence off her nipple. Oh fuck. That just pushed her arousal higher. Answer him? What was the question again? Oh yeah, had she masturbated. She groaned, knowing he'd stop if she didn't answer.

"Yes. I did."

"And did you think of me as you rubbed at your little clit? Or did you use a toy on yourself? Did you play with your nipples and think about the way I suckled on them?" His voice was low, husky as he questioned her and it sent waves of arousal shivering across her skin.

"Yes! Yes!" she cried out as he continued to lick at her nipple.

"And did it feel as good as when I had my tongue against your clit, licking you like you're my favorite treat?"

"No. No, it didn't feel nearly as good." Nothing came close to when he touched her.

"Tell me what you want," he demanded.

"You. Inside me."

He shook his head with a smile. "No, not yet. Not until you're mad with arousal."

"I'm mad with arousal now!" she protested.

"I don't think so. You've got a way to go yet." He kissed his way down her tummy. "Pull your legs up to your chest and hold them there."

She couldn't believe the things he demanded of her. And yet, she didn't want it any other way. She loved when he took command. She drew her legs up to her chest, holding them there.

He lay on his stomach, his face inches from her pussy. He ran his finger along the top of her pussy. "I can see you kept up your grooming. That's very nice. But from now on, Daddy takes care of all your personal grooming, understand?"

"Yes, Daddy."

"Good girl. Now keep hold of your legs, but spread them wide for me."

She whimpered as she spread her legs, putting herself completely on display for him.

"Pretty, pretty pussy." He patted it softly then leaned in and ran his tongue along the slit.

Her legs trembled. Not that she was getting tired or cramped in this position but because she wanted more. Needed more.

Parting her lips, he pressed his tongue against her clit, just holding it there. Then he started to push a finger inside her, even further than he had before. It was tight, it burned, and she started to wonder for the first time just how this was going to work.

"Shh," he told her. "I'm going to look after you, Ellie. All you need to do is what I tell you. Let me take care of everything else. Good girl. Relax."

It was pretty impossible to relax when his tongue lapped at her clit. Oh God. Shit. It felt unbelievably good. Too good. She wanted it to last forever, yet she knew it wouldn't take much to make her come.

"Oh. Oh. More. Please, more."

He had two fingers partially inside her passage, stretching her. "That's it, little girl. Stretch for me. Damn, you are going to feel so tight around my cock. You come whenever you like. That's it. Come for me now."

The first ripple ran over her, a small precursor. Then her

orgasm slammed into her like a steam engine, robbing her of her ability to breathe, to think. She dropped her hold on her legs, no longer able to keep them in place. But Bear moved onto his knees and pressed her legs back with his body as he leaned over her, his weight resting on his hands on either side of her. His cock nudged her entrance. Reaching down, he grasped hold of the shaft and guided himself inside her.

She was still rocking from the effects of that mind-blowing orgasm and it took her a moment to register the feeling of being stretched. Of being full. Too full. Then he gave a sudden thrust, breaking past the barrier of her virginity.

She let out a scream. And this wasn't one of pleasure. Oh fuck, that hurt. It hurt so bad.

"Shh, baby girl. It's okay. It's all over now."

"That hurt!" she wailed. Tears dripped down her face. She knew it would hurt, but she'd never figured it would be that bad. Her insides burned and throbbed. How could this be pleasurable?

"I know, sweetheart. But it's all over now. Shh, don't cry. You're breaking my heart."

It took her awhile to calm herself. The burning was starting to fade as she realized this couldn't be all that comfortable for him, laying there with his cock inside her. She needed to get her shit together.

"I'm sorry, you can move if you want."

He gave a chuckle. "Baby, I'm not moving until you stop crying. Hush, now. Give me your breast. Let Daddy make it all okay."

She offered up her breast to him and he had to bend to reach it since he was so much bigger than her. He suckled gently on her nipple. Pleasure trickled through her body. His sucking became stronger and she groaned as she felt an answering tug in her clit. Then he moved to her other nipple, doing the same. And suddenly she wanted him to move. She wanted to feel him come inside her. She pushed her hips up.

"More," she groaned.

"Does my baby want me to fuck her?" he murmured in a husky voice that sent a shiver across her skin.

"Yes, please."

He grinned. "Always so polite. Such a good girl, aren't you? My good, dirty girl. Fuck, I love you."

He drew his cock out of her tight passage as he talked, going slowly, then he pushed himself deep. As he moved, the hurt morphed into something else. With each thrust, he hit a spot inside her that sent sparks of desire through her blood. He reached between them to rub at her clit.

"Do you need to come again, baby girl?" he asked her.

"Yes. Oh yes please!"

"So hot. So tight. Fuck, you make me lose control so easily."

Her breasts bobbed with each thrust and he groaned as he stared down at them. "Perfect breasts, beautiful face and the most loving personality of anyone I've ever met. And mine, all mine."

"All yours. Now please, make me come!"

He grinned. "Your wish is my command."

He moved harder. Faster. Her pleasure bloomed then exploded in a rush that left her shaking beneath him, her cries filling the room. He placed both hands on the mattress and fucked her. There was no other word for it. She wrapped her legs around his waist and just held on for the ride.

Oh, and what a ride it was. Sweat coated their bodies. Their breaths came in sharp pants. The muscles in his neck were tight, his jaw clenched as he drove himself deep inside her.

"I'm so close, baby girl. So close."

She kissed her way along his chest, sucking one nipple into her mouth. He came with a shout, stilling, his breath coming in raw, hard pants. She ran her hand up and down his back, as though trying to soothe him.

"So good. Shit," he muttered. Slowly, he withdrew from her.

Now that the adrenaline was fading, she was aware that she felt a little tender down there. But when he rolled to his side and tucked her into his side, she decided she didn't care.

Because this was perfect. This was where she was meant to be. This was home.

EPILOGUE

"Where are your glasses, little girl?" Daddy asked in a low rumble as he put a sippy cup filled with water beside her on the floor.

Uh-oh.

"Umm, I'm not sure, Daddy," she said as she concentrated on her drawing.

A big hand reached down and plucked the colored pencil she'd been using out of her hand.

"Hey, Daddy, I was using that." She glared up at him.

"You shouldn't be doing any drawing without your glasses on," he rumbled back at her. "You know Doc said you need them for reading and drawing."

"Doc's mean."

Daddy raised an eyebrow. "Why? Because he said it's perfectly safe for Daddy to spank you now?"

"Yes. Mean."

Turned out Doc was right and her headaches had been related to her eyesight. Since getting her glasses, her headaches had all but disappeared. Just yesterday, Doc had given her a clean bill of health. He'd also told Bear he was free to spank her ass as often as was required. She'd poked her tongue out at him for that, which had resulted in Bear giving her a couple of swats right there in front of him.

"Seems to me the ban on spanking ended just in time," he told her mildly. "You still haven't answered me. Where are your glasses?"

"I really don't know. I can't find them." She glanced to see how upset he was with her.

He just heaved out a breath. "You lost them again?"

She chewed at her lip. "Uh-huh, I'm sorry, Daddy."

"I swear I'm going to find some way to secure them to your clothing like they do with pacifiers."

"I'm not a baby, Daddy!" she informed him haughtily.

"Where have you been today that you might have lost them?"

"To see Doc."

"No. We brought them back with us. I remember putting them in your case on the shelf, where they are supposed to be kept when you're not using them." He gave her a stern look.

She bit her lip, looking up at the shelf. The case was there, but not the glasses.

"Maybe the bad fairies stole them," she suggested, bouncing up and down slightly, pleased with herself for thinking of that.

"Bad fairies, huh? Or maybe they were left somewhere by one naughty girl who can't seem to keep track of her possessions?"

Her shoulders slumped. "I'm sorry, Daddy."

He crouched in front of her. "It's okay, baby. Daddy knows you don't mean to keep losing them."

Well, maybe there was a part of her that wouldn't mind saying goodbye to them permanently. She hated wearing them. But she hated the headaches more.

"Drink your water," he commanded.

She wrinkled her nose at the sippy cup. "Can I have juice, Daddy?"

"Nope, you know Doc wants you to drink more water. Drink. Or you'll be sitting on a sore bottom and still having to drink your water."

She sighed. "Fine."

"Watch the attitude, young lady."

She stuck her tongue out at him. He raised one eyebrow, giving her *the look*. *The look* meant she'd pushed him too far. Uh-oh. She stood. She had no idea where she was planning on running to, but before she could move, he'd grabbed hold of her. He pulled a chair out from the small dining table, then put his foot up on the seat before tipping her over his wide thigh.

Before she could protest, he had delivered a flurry of smacks to her ass. They weren't particularly hard. More to catch her attention than anything else. But by the time he'd placed her back on her feet, her bottom stung.

She reached around to rub and he crossed his arms over his chest, giving her a pointed look. "I wouldn't, baby girl. Not unless you want to spend some time in the corner."

Nope, she didn't want that. She pouted but put her arms back at her sides. "That was mean, Daddy."

"Sticking your tongue out at Daddy and giving him sass wasn't very nice, either, was it?" he countered.

She shook her head, sniffling. "No. Sorry, Daddy."

He ran his hand over her head. "I love you, little girl. I'm so glad you're here with me."

She threw herself into his arms. "Me too." There was nowhere else she'd rather be. Bear took such good care of her. He was her daddy, her best friend, her lover and protector. When she'd decided to call her parents and let them know she was all right, he'd stood right next to her, one arm wrapped around her. And when her mother had told her never to call again, that she was dead to them, he'd held her as she'd cried.

"Tell me what you're drawing," he said, glancing down at the picture.

"Guess," she replied with a grin.

There was silence and she had to hold back a giggle. Poor Daddy, he had no idea what he was looking at. And she liked to tease him sometimes.

"Well, Daddy? What is it?"

"It's a masterpiece, is what it is." He leaned in and kissed the top of her head.

She giggled. "You always say that."

"We're going to need a bigger fridge to put all your master-pieces on." He took the picture from her and hung it up proudly. In the beginning, she'd been embarrassed that someone might see. Her Little side was just for Daddy. But very few people ever came into their cabin, and those that had seen the pictures she'd drawn hadn't even blinked.

And as she'd gotten to know everyone on the ranch, she'd grown less worried that they might judge or ridicule her. Every man here seemed intent on making her feel as comfortable as possible. They were also all overly protective.

But that was kind of sweet. Except for when they tattled on her.

She loved living here, in their little cabin. Bear had told her that they could move into a bigger one, but she didn't really want to. This place was cozy and sweet. Bear worked a lot during the day, but when he came home, he gave all of his attention to her. It was amazing. She'd been so lonely, starved for affection and now she had all the attention she could desire.

She hadn't been able to patch things up with her parents, but at least she'd tried. And she had a new family now.

"All right, so back to your glasses. Did you go anywhere else after I brought you back here from visiting Doc?"

She sighed. "I went to visit the horses, but only for a little while."

"Is that so?" he drawled.

Uh-oh.

"Someone tattled, didn't they? Who was it? Linc?"

"It doesn't matter who. I told you to take a nap. How long after I put you down did you get up and go down to the stables?"

"I didn't look at the time, Daddy."

He snorted. "I bet you didn't. That was naughty of you, Ellie."

"I wasn't tired, Daddy. I just wanted to go give Eagle a few treats." Eagle was Bear's horse and she loved him. But Bear wouldn't let her ride him. He wanted her to learn to ride on a gentler horse. She didn't think Eagle would like her riding another horse, though.

"He's going to get fat on all the treats you give him," he said dryly.

"He gets lonely. He likes me visiting."

"He does. And you can visit whenever you like. But only if I haven't given you orders to rest or stay in the cabin." He crossed his arms over his chest and leaned back against the counter of the small kitchen area. They didn't cook in here, but took all their meals in the main dining hall, which was just as well since she was such a terrible cook. "And only if you dress appropriately and stick to the main paths. No wandering off."

"I didn't wander off," she protested.

"Clint is threatening to put a GPS tracker on you," he told her. "I'm in agreement."

"Get lost a few times and suddenly everyone wants to track you." She threw her hands up in the air.

"A few times? You've been here for less than three weeks and you've wandered off five times!"

"I'm sure I'll get better at navigating my way around."

He pointed a finger at her. "I'm not so sure. Do you remember your rules about walking around the ranch?"

"I have to keep to the main paths and carry my cell phone everywhere," she replied.

A sudden knock on the door had her turning with a gasp. She looked down at herself. She was dressed in the onesie Bear had ordered for her online. It had just arrived today. It was grey and white; the hood had a pair of ears and a rabbit face. It even had a fluffy tail at the back.

Lots of adults wore onesies like this nowadays. Of course, they didn't all have back flaps that made it easier for Daddy to reach her bottom. But the person at the door didn't need to know that.

She still blushed slightly as Bear opened the door. Linc stood on the other side.

"Linc," Bear said with a nod.

"Hey, Bear. Found these down by Eagle's stall. Figured your girl might need them." Linc handed Bear a pair of glasses and looked down at her with a smile. "Hey there, sweetheart. You look cute tonight."

She smiled shyly. "Thank you."

"Thanks, Linc. Appreciate it."

"No problem."

Bear turned after shutting the door and held up her glasses. He moved to the case and grabbed the cloth to clean them, then put them away.

"See, I knew they'd be found in the end," she said cheerfully.

He gave her a firm look.

"Are you mad at me for losing the glasses, Daddy?"

"You know I'm not. But we do have a couple of punishments to take care of, don't we?"

"We do?" she asked with fake innocence.

"You know full well that Daddy hasn't yet punished you for not going to the doctor when you promised."

Drat. She figured he might have forgotten that. Yeah, she should have known she didn't have that sort of luck.

"I've been waiting until Doc gave the all clear to spank you. I'm also not happy that you disobeyed me today and got up after I put you down for a nap. Now, I want you to go and brush your teeth and go to the toilet then come back in here."

She dragged her steps as she got up and went into the small attached bathroom. She turned back to give him a pleading look. "But, Daddy, you already spanked me tonight. Can't that be enough?"

"Those few pats I gave you wouldn't have even hurt. Certainly not enough to make an impression on you. Now git. You have five minutes. No dawdling. Since you missed your nap, you're going to bed early."

Well, that just sucked. But she walked into the bathroom and brushed her teeth then used the toilet. She really wanted to delay the inevitable spanking, but she knew he'd just come in and drag her out and then he'd probably give her extras. She covered her bottom reflexively.

"Little girl, time's up."

"Coming." She walked into the main room of the cabin to find him sitting on the sofa.

"Come here." He pointed at the floor between his legs. She walked over and stood between his knees. He cupped her face between his big hands. "Do you know why you're getting punished?"

"Because I've been a bad, bad girl," she said with a pout.

He just shook his head, but she caught a glimpse of a smile. "You're not a bad girl. But you are my girl. And I'm going to do whatever it takes to look after you."

"You do a great job of that already, without the spankings."

He shook his head. "No, baby. You can't talk me out of this. I'm sorry it's been so long for you to wait to receive your discipline. But after your spanking, everything is wiped clean. Understand?" He patted his lap. "Over you go."

She looked down at his lap and then over at the door and then down at his lap again.

"Think you'd make it far, baby?" he asked, sounding more amused than anything else.

"I reckon I could make it out the door," she told him.

"And I reckon that would mean you'd get a spanking right where I caught you. No matter who was around."

She wrinkled her nose. Then with a sigh she climbed over his lap. He was sitting in the middle of the couch. So, her body and legs ended up on either side of his lap, supported by the couch. He pulled down the back flap of her onesie, revealing her bare bottom.

"No panties, good girl." He rubbed her bottom. "Going to have to get more of these onesies. This back flap makes it very easy to spank you."

She groaned at those words.

"Comfortable, baby?" he asked.

She snorted. "Is it really possible for somebody who is about to get a spanking to be comfortable?"

"You know what I mean," he said to her. "I want the only discomfort to be in your bottom."

"I'm fine, Daddy." He was as protective as always.

He started gently, which surprised her. But it wasn't long until the smacks grew harder, faster. Tears dripped down her face as she sobbed. She kicked her feet, trying to wriggle her way off his lap.

She reached back, unable to stop herself, needing to do something to protect her poor bottom from more punishment. Already her butt was stinging. Instead of grabbing her hands as she'd expected, he shifted position, moving forward on the sofa. Was he stopping? Was it over? She had to admit that even though the spanking hurt, it wasn't as bad as she'd been imagining.

But no, he just half-turned her so she lay more over his left hip, her legs straddling his wide thigh. He secured her left leg between his, spreading her legs wide.

Then he tugged the onesie down further and started spanking the tender skin of her thighs. He moved from one thigh to the other. Oh God, that damn well hurt!

"Please stop!" She couldn't stop herself from begging him. The pain was immense. He covered her ass with more hard smacks of his palm. Sobs rocked her body, tears dripped down her face.

"Daddy! Please!" she cried as he laid smack after smack on her throbbing bottom. It felt like it had swollen to twice its size. She wasn't going to sit for a week after this!

"Next time you promise to do something, I want you to remember this. What the consequences are for breaking a promise. For disobeying Daddy." Each word was emphasized with a smack to her ass.

The spanks stopped. Oh, thank God. Then he leaned over, his chest brushing against her sore bottom.

What was he doing?

"Daddy, can I move?"

He shifted back into the couch, moving her into her previous position over his lap, but this time he had both of her legs secured between his. "No, because I'm not finished yet. I want you to know how serious I am about your health. You promised to go to the doctor. Twice you told me you would go. That means that I'm going to use more than my hand for this spanking, to make you aware of just how serious I am about your health."

More than his hand? She turned to look at him, and her breath caught in her chest as she saw he held his belt in his hand. No. No, no, no.

"No, Daddy!" She tried to fight her way free of his hold, but he held her steady.

"I'm sorry, baby. But you're getting a few licks of the belt."

She sobbed. "It will hurt too much!"

"Easy, sweetheart. I'd never give you more than you can take. Since this is your first experience with the belt, I'm going to go very easy on you and just give you five. Give me both of your hands. I don't want you trying to reach back."

"Daddy, please don't," she begged.

"Hands, little girl, or it's ten with the belt."

Oh God. Five already sounded dire enough. She put her hands back and he secured her wrists with one hand, pressing down on her back to hold her still. Then the belt landed. A fiery stripe erupted across her buttocks.

She howled. She couldn't help it. Her bottom was already tender. This was too much. She couldn't take it.

Another stripe landed. Her breath hitched. She couldn't even scream this time. Couldn't cry. It felt like someone had branded her.

Another one. By the time the fourth landed, her frozen state had disappeared and she screamed. Her sobs rocked her body. The fifth came down and she was lost to the tears. She collapsed on his lap. He turned her gently and picked her up, carrying her to the bed and positioning her on her side. Then he lay next to her, facing her, engulfing her in his arms.

"Shh, baby. Good girl. My good little girl. Shh, I know it hurts. You're all right. It's all over."

"I...I'm...sorry...Daddy," she managed to get out between sobs. It felt like her bottom was on fire.

"I know, baby. I know. Me too. I don't enjoy having to cause you such pain, but I want you to know that you are so important to me. You are everything. I can never lose you." He brushed her hair off her face then leaned in and kissed away her tears.

"You never will." She sniffled. "Can I have Jeremiah Bear Junior?"

He sighed. "I still can't believe you called him that."

"What's wrong with calling him that?" He'd hated that name from the start.

He grimaced, but didn't say anything.

She stared up at him then it dawned on her. "Wait. I can't believe I never guessed it. That's your name, isn't it?" Sounded kind of silly, but with everything else going on, she'd kind of given up on figuring out his real name.

He groaned and lay on his back, running his hand over his face.

"It is. Isn't it? Your name is Jeremiah. Why wouldn't you tell me that?"

"Because I hate the name," he muttered.

"Wait. You've got the same name as my first teddy. My Aunt Rose sent him to look after me. I wonder if she sent you too."

He stared up at her as she leaned up on one elbow beside him. "You're my guardian angel."

"I might be your guardian, but I'm certainly no angel." He reached up and brushed her hair back over her shoulder. "Your Aunt Rose is your guardian angel. I'm the man who loves you, the daddy who adores you, and I'm going to look after you the way she would have wanted me too."

She snuggled against him. "I'm not so sure she would approve of the spanking."

He grinned. "Oh, I don't know. I think she'd definitely approve."

He ran his hand up and down her back. "I love you, baby girl."

"I love you too, Daddy." She sent a quick thanks up to Aunt Rose for sending Ellie her very own Daddy Bear.

THANKS FOR READING Bear and Ellie's story, I hope you enjoyed it! Clint and Charlie's story is coming August, 1ˢᵗ in Daddy's Little Darling.

DADDY'S LITTLE DARLING

Montana Daddies, book 2

She was desperate, homeless and alone...

Charlie was used to fending for herself. She wasn't necessarily that good at it, considering she was currently living in her car, but it was the only life she knew. She didn't have family, or friends and she certainly wasn't used to anyone caring about what she did.

Then she takes a temporary job on Sanctuary Ranch, where the men are all dominant and alpha and the woman are cherished and protected. And suddenly there are rules, and consequences for breaking them, and she isn't certain how she feels about that. Considering the man acting as her guardian is also her boss, and the sexiest, most dominant man she's ever met.

He's blunt, gruff and used to getting his way...

Clint likes to be in control. Craves it. What he doesn't like are surprises. And that's exactly what she is. A complete and utter shock to the system. She's in need of a protector, of a Daddy to take care of her.

But that someone can't be him.

Contains one totally Alpha Daddy Dom and a woman who manages to tug at his every protective instinct.

Printed in Great Britain
by Amazon

25411487R00108